Ward of the State
Larry Giordano's Life as a Foster Kid

Jeff Ives

with

Larry Giordano

DEDICATION

To my wife Eileen and my children—Marie Jean and husband John and my grandson Jack, Lonnie and his wife Stacy and daughter Amelia, and Stephen and his wife Danielle and their children Rocco and Arden—whose understanding and encouragement mean so much to me. They have given me a family any man would be proud of.

4

ACKNOWLEDGMENTS

I wish to express my appreciation to Jeff Ives, the writer of this book, who dedicated himself to the research and development of this story. To my Foster Mother, Helen Giordano, to whom I am so grateful for giving me a home and family to call my own. And to my God, who has watched over me since I was born and guided my life toward the wonderful events that made me who I am today.

AUTHOR'S NOTE

This book tells the actual events of Larry Giordano's life growing up as a foster child. It is best considered a biographical novel since some of the names and details have been changed for the sake of the narrative.

Early in the morning on May 8, 1945, a slight, 20-year-old woman with a sweet face checked out of the Hotel Kimball in Springfield, Massachusetts. She dropped her key off and thanked the clerk in broken English. Her hands shook as she pushed through heavy glass doors and emerged into the chilly morning air outside. Her mind was made up, but frayed at the edges. Her eyes wandered up the brown brick facade to the windows above. Behind one of those windows lay her infant son on an empty bed. She paused, as if listening to hear his cries, a sound she could feel in the back of her mind. But there was nothing beyond her thoughts to reveal what she was doing. He never cried that much, she thought to herself, thinking of the baby in the past tense—as if she had already left and been gone for years. She turned, walked to the station and boarded a train to Boston.

The passenger car swayed into movement and rumbled down the tracks. She thought back to through the blur of moments that had brought her to this one over years of growing up in Quebec under the unyielding control of her domineering grandmother. She ran away from home. She crossed the U.S. border saying that she was going to visit relatives. At the Army base in Maine, she met the tall, handsome mechanic. Their time together was short and he was shipped off to war. Things became more confusing every day. She was pregnant. She had no money. Her family would not understand, and with nobody to turn to, she replied to an employment ad in Boston and found herself at the large front doors of a wealthy couple. They took her on as a maid and advised her about her situation. She attended some birthing classes between performing her duties at the house.

When the time came, her employer drove her to Saint

Elizabeth's Hospital in Boston on a warm spring afternoon and dropped her off. She gave birth to a healthy baby boy. Her son nestled beside her in the hospital room as she recovered for the next two weeks, the longest amount of time the two would ever spend together. She told the nurses that she was taking her baby to see family in Maine. The head nurse walked the mother and son to the train station and bought her a ticket on the Maine line. As soon as the nurse was out of sight, the ticket was traded in for another one to Springfield, Massachusetts.

The train ride out to Springfield had felt like the opening climb of a roller coaster. Each clack of the wheels on the tracks, each jostle of the baby's small head in the crook of her arm, haunted her with the unbearable suspense of knowing what she was about to do. Yet, she saw no other way. Checking in at the hotel desk under a false name was simpler than she had thought it would be. The night in the hotel room was sleepless. She paced back and forth as the baby shifted innocently in its hospital blankets until the morning sun came. Twice she walked to the door, held the handle, and turned back to look at him. The second time, she turned the handle and stepped out alone. The door shut behind her.

Later that morning, the hotel clerk absently mentioned to his manager about how the girl with the baby had checked out, but it was funny that he didn't remember seeing the baby with her. The manager rushed to the third-floor room, unlocked the door, and swung it open to find a healthy but hungry infant sobbing on the bed. The police were called and the baby was taken to a local hospital, where the nurses fawned over him, telling eager newspaper reporters how excellent he was and what a wonderful temperament he had. They took pictures of him for the paper, but he needed a name. Wire services were alight with news that the Nazis had signed an unconditional surrender that officially ended the war in Europe. So the nurses took to calling the child "Victor," reflecting their joy at seeing this new baby boy with the celebratory images on the front pages of every newspaper showing soldiers and sailors welcoming an end to five years of fighting across the Atlantic.

His mother was quickly found and apprehended by the police, who tracked her down using the baby's blankets. It turned out that the nurses hadn't believed that this young mother had family in Maine to visit. They had marked the blankets with their hospital number just in case, and they weren't the least bit surprised when the police called about the abandoned baby.

The Springfield newspapers continued to call him Victor, even after his mother officially named the baby Lawrence Gagnon during the legal proceedings that led up to her being deported back to her family in Quebec. She and her family refused to take Lawrence home to Canada. Instead, he was designated #32590A by the Massachusetts Department of Child Guardianship as a ward of the state.

Like most children under the care of the state, Lawrence Gagnon spent time at an orphanage in before being taken to a foster home for infants in Roxbury. He was watched carefully and fed regularly by a combination of caretakers, doctors, and nurses. They remarked to each other about his quiet temperament; his slight frame; and his wide, beautiful eyes. When the time came, he was taken away from all of them by a social worker with the State's Division of Child Guardianship and brought to a new home—60 Dean Street in Everett.

The tall blue house stretched back from a quiet street with patches of grass out front and a small yard fenced around the back. The lady of the house was Helen Giordano. She was a tall, stately woman with olive skin and the firm features of a kindhearted person who had learned not to back down from anyone. She was the proud mother of four children: Billy, Rosemary, Benny, and Clara. After successfully raising them, she decided that there was more parenting left inside her so, in 1948, she greeted a bundled-up three-year-old boy on the brick steps in front. She stood with the social worker, watching the boy toddle around his new surroundings and glance at them as he explored the sun-soaked porch surrounded by an ornate railing. Helen smiled fondly at him and opened the front door, and the boy grinned back and bounced inside. Helen watched him sink comfortably into a seat on the living room rug and gave him an approving wink. She whispered under her breath, "Welcome home Larry."

Swan Street Park was dark. The streetlights were out. On any other night, that would mean the kids who called this baseball diamond, basketball court, and playground in Everett home were in bed. (Especially in the winter.) During the summer, the streetlights stayed on until 9 or 10 o'clock, and with their light came the echoes of boys on third base calling "Out!" and girls laughing from their perch on the chain-link fence surrounding the dusty infield. In the summer, only complaining neighbors, threatening cops, and mothers announcing the evening meal by shouting "Dinnah!" from their doorways could quiet the sounds of Swan Street Park.

The frozen air brought quiet to the baseball diamond. The few kids who did brave a night out in the winter were there to watch their breath rise into the sky as they made plans to hop on trolleys, find a few other guys to round out a game at the pool hall, or knock on other kids' doors to find a warm place to hang out. It was typically too cold to last long outside. In the winter at this time of night, no sounds should have been detected at Swan Street Park.

But it was New Year's Eve, and the usual silence was broken by the soft sounds of scraped shuffling. Quiet broke with what sounded like a dozen brooms bristling down the frost-coated street. The sound got louder and louder as figures appeared, approaching the dark center of the park. Each figure emerged as a boy. They wore tattered coats, most a couple sizes too small. A few had scarves knotted around their necks. Fewer still had hats or gloves. They trudged toward the park with purpose—and a burden. Each boy strained proudly under the load of a Christmas tree.

The dry branches shed their needles along the frozen path. From every direction and every cross street, timed like a military operation, the boys poured into the park and dropped their trees underneath the rusty iron monkey bars. The larger boys arrived first, turned, and watched the rest. The straggling smaller boys passed through the gap in the chain-link fence, the load of each tree weighing heavily on their little legs. The older kids would send them on a continued mission for more. The stacking began.

The trees were piled, bent, and wrapped around the park's monkey bars until it looked like a massive oblong wreath. The pine tar covered their fingers and the pine smell filled their nostrils. And when every curb has been relieved of its Christmas trees, and when the monkey bars were bursting with dry evergreen, a nervous

12

excitement descended into the pack of kids. They muttered to each other in the cold. The older kids smiled confidently. The younger kids practiced acting tough, feigning that it was no big deal; they did this all the time.

Then the cop pulled up. He had been just down the street the whole time. The older boys watched him. They had expected him and they knew what to do. The younger kids stopped fidgeting and stood at nervous attention. They slowed down their breathing to allow the fewest visible puffs of air. The older boys knew that cop couldn't stay there forever. The younger boys tried to believe it too, muttering hopefully under their breath. The wait went on.

It was a lose/lose situation for the cop, and the older boys knew it. He could sit there all night and watch them do nothing. Or, he could get out of his cruiser and walk over to the park, only to watch the gang scatter back into the neighborhood without the chance to identify a single kid. Then he could stand there alone with a pile of Christmas trees. No, the cop always knew what was going on. Every year it was the same ritual. He watched them and they watched him. Somewhere deep down he remembered a New Year's Eve when he was young. He gave up, swore under his breath, and drove away. The boys watched him go, brake lights fading down the hill, and then sprung into action.

A nickel bought a can of lighter fluid. Matches were free everywhere. The trees crinkled pleasingly under the dowsing stream of acrid gas, and the tallest, most senior, boy stepped forward, thumb on a match against the lighting strip. He grinned and turned toward each red, expectant face.

"Welcome to 1952, boys."

The match was struck and dropped in an instant, bursting tall, blue flames and sparks. For half a second, the boys watched the rising spectacle, their faces reflecting back the hot beams of raging fire. And then they all shouted, "RUN!"

It was scattershot mayhem at its best. The first two boys to reach the corner fire alarm had the reward of yanking down each frozen white handle, sounding a loud, long, whining horn that sent for the fire department. Lights were flicked in the surrounding houses as curious faces peeked from windows to see the flames rising up from the park. In moments, the boys were gone. Most of them were already home, safely listening with giddy excitement for the oncoming fire trucks.

13

The Swan Street Rats had struck again.

One of those Swan Street Rats was seven-year-old Larry Gagnon. His thin, lanky body was bundled in a coarse wool sweater over his plaid shirt and corduroy pants. Thick socks kept his feet warm in his canvas sneakers and he wore a wool cap to cover his bowl-cut brown hair. He paused briefly at the edge of the park to take in the whole chaotic scene, the thrill of inevitable sirens followed by his friends racing home through the neighborhood. His sharp eyes flashed from side to side, keeping lookout for the fire engines as he watched the other kids disappear into the lattice-like network of side streets and backyards. When the coast was clear, he set out for his home on Dean Street.

It was farther away from the park than some of the other boys had to go. Larry sprinted to the corner, hopped a small garden fence, and slipped through a hedge just as the sirens drew close. He got up onto the porch and flew through the side door and into the stairway of his house. He hesitated before heading completely inside. The memory of dozens of ambushes at the foot of these stairs haunted his resolve. This was usually where he got caught red-handed coming home late by his foster mother, or as he called her, "Mum." She might have been behind the door, waiting with a thumb and forefinger ready to clamp down on his left ear. She could have already followed him through the side door to come up the staircase from behind, wielding her weapon of choice—the dreaded green broom.

Mrs. Giordano was no slouch, and Larry knew it. Lots of parents say they have two sets of eyes, with the second set in the back of their heads, but Mrs. Giordano actually did. She also had eyes on every street lamp, in the walls, at the movie theater, and most inconveniently, at the park. He was sure she knew what the Swan Street Rats had just done. He was almost completely sure that the sound of fire trucks charging toward the park was a dead giveaway. So, the only mystery left for Larry was when she was going to nab him, not if.

For any other seven-year-old kid, the prospect of being attacked by a large, broom-wielding woman on a dark staircase after running from the scene of an illegal bonfire would be terrifying. But Larry was tough. He gritted his teeth, grabbed the knob to the inside door and turned. It was unlocked. The door opened with a careful nudge. He braced himself for her swift hand to snatch him up … but nothing came. The upstairs hallway was empty too.

Larry didn't pause to question his good fortune. He sprang forward, avoiding the familiar spots in the floor that creaked. He slipped silently into his small corner room, shuffled past the bat and glove leaning against the dresser, and dove beneath his covers fully clothed. The kerosene smell of the fire was still in his nostrils. He listened to the din of sirens only blocks away and realized that he had gotten away with it. For the first time that night, Larry smiled.

Downstairs, Helen Giordano sipped her tea. She was wearing a long, cream-colored overcoat with a pair of brown leather boots, just in case she needed to go running out the door after Larry. Her dark, curly hair was done up in a bun with a flowered band around it. Her thin, round glasses covered dark brown eyes and helped snap the soft-lit room into focus. Her olive skin had a few small wrinkles, but she looked remarkably young and healthy, considering the maelstrom of raucous children she'd been surrounded by for decades—starting with her own and now the foster children. She thrived on the work of caring for them all. Some were more challenging than others. Larry was one of the ones she worried about most.

Helen had been up all evening, waiting for Larry to get home. The streetlights went out at 7 o'clock. He didn't sneak up the backstairs until 10. It sounded as if half the fire department was at the park. She knew exactly what had been going on. She'd raised two boys in this neighborhood already, and there were no surprises. In any other circumstance, she would have had a broomstick in her hand and answers from the boy. But not tonight.

Tonight, she chose to do nothing, except be glad Larry was safe. The pale blue of drapery and furniture in the living room had fallen into shadow hours ago while she watched the sun go down waiting for him. She had more concern for Larry than anyone knew. Her vigorous appearance shone out to others as pure, unwavering composure. On the outside, she appeared to be made of the same strong wrought iron that circled the porch of her house. On the inside, she nursed the heart of a woman who had taken on the responsibility of being Larry's mother. On the inside, she was afraid, and she had been for the four years since Larry had arrived to stay with her.

She knew that other foster children came and went. Their parents made progress with the state, with the law. Other foster children went back and stayed with their real family for weeks, months, or even forever. Not Larry. Larry was different. Larry was with her for good. How many times did she reassure him? How many times had the state agent reassured him? He wasn't going to be taken away from Helen's house. He still got nervous about being sent away.

Helen often wondered what Larry thought brought him to her. His quiet features had never let on that he cared about anything but food in the morning, baseball all day, supper at night, and sneaking to bed without taking a bath. If he ever questioned why he was living with her and not someone with his same last name, Gagnon, he never let on. He didn't ask about it. She decided Larry knew that names didn't matter. This was their life now. His responsibility was to avoid her wrath at all costs. Her responsibility was to keep him safe.

That was easier said than done. She had watched Larry grow from a wayward toddler to a charming little rascal. He had started in isolation, staying close to the house, playing in the yard with the other kids that lived with Helen. Gradually, he had wandered out into the neighborhood, making friends farther away. She did not hesitate to snap at anyone who threatened him, including the adults who called him "state ward" as he walked by. When she heard that, she marched right up to them, stared them in the face, and explained in no uncertain terms that this boy belonged here; their judgment was not accepted.

Nowadays, he typically joined up with his pack of boys down at Swan Street Park. Helen watched him come home every day with a strange mixture of pride and fear. She was proud to see this skinny little man, scuffed up with dirt from the infield after a day of rough-and-tumble fun. She was afraid because she knew at least one of those kids in the park would end up in a bad situation someday, either with the law or with each other. That kid could be Larry. It was a numbers game. She felt like the sentinel on watch.

She was going to make sure, no matter what, that Larry was not that child who people clucked about with disappointment, the child who went out one day and didn't come back. The odds were already stacked against him.

When those neighbors, leaning up against the fence, called him the "state ward," they were pushing him to the outside, casting him out. She didn't have much in the way of resources to protect him. She couldn't be there every time to try and stop them, and she couldn't afford to give him the right clothes, sports equipment, or bike to help him fit in. A holiday check from the state and a stipend covered a pair of yearly sneakers, an annual clothes-shopping expedition to Boston, and not much more for the growing boy. She had to do the rest. She had to harness her will to guide him on the right path. And she had to pray that her powers as a mother were strong enough to see him through.

Helen took another sip of tea. The commotion at the park was over. No more sirens. Whatever the boys did, they didn't do any lasting damage, she thought. The clock chimed midnight and she went up to bed, gently closing Larry's door as she passed. Tonight he did something in the park that brought in the fire department. He would be hearing from her about that, of course. "Once in a while, I can let him sleep before he gets it," she thought.

After all, it was New Year's Day.

Early morning in Everett came complete with the sound of milk deliveries and low-flying jets clearing Logan Airport. Larry woke up to the dull roar and shaking walls of one of those take-offs. He pulled on a fresh pair of pants, thick socks, his canvas sneakers, a plain white t-shirt, and his thickest grey sweater. The sun was out and he was hoping to get away with not wearing his tattered winter jacket. It felt too small, and he was looking to dress like the older kids. Then he bounded down the stairs to find Mrs. Giordano lighting the gas for hot water.

He was relieved to see that her broom was nowhere in sight. "Morning, Larry," she said absently as he sat down. Larry glanced at her from the table. Mrs. Giordano glanced back.

"Ya hear those fire trucks?" she asked, turning to get a better look at Larry's widening eyes as he thought about her question. He knew better than to say anything back. Instead he shuffled to the other side of the white painted bench at the kitchen table and glanced out the window casually. Helen watched him, and then continued talking.

"Louise says the park kids burned up all the Christmas trees, Larry," she said, referring to their neighbor who always seems to know the scuttlebutt. Larry still gave no reaction. Helen set the orange juice bottle and some glasses down on the table. Larry poured himself some for himself while watching her cautiously. She continued speaking in a slow, deliberate, slightly threatening tone. "Good thing you're too young to get mixed up in something like that."

She placed some toast and butter on the table. Larry took a piece and, for a long time, the only sound in the room was the scraping of his butter knife as he sat nervously on the edge of the bench. He glanced toward the window and wondered if he could possibly open it and jump out, should the need arise. Finally he spoke.

"Where's Ruthie at?" he asked. Ruthie was another one of Helen's charges. She was the same age as Larry. She had her own brand of rebellion. She and Larry were inseparable since they came to the house. Each one thought the other got away with more.

"She's down at the store with Clara," Helen said. "They're opening up together." Clara was Helen's tall, soft-spoken daughter. Her brown hair and kind eyes were a welcome presence around the house, especially if Helen was on the warpath. Clara worked at Carroll Cut-Rate, a convenience store downtown. Ruthie tagged along with her to help out when she was on shift. Larry finished off his toast and slid off the bench and under the table toward the counter, where he grabbed a hard-boiled egg with the clear intent to take it with him out the door.

"I better go down and help them out," Larry said through his filled mouth, edging toward the exit. Helen's reaction was instantaneous and impressive. Her heavy hand slammed into the counter with a deafening thud that shook the house. She spun forward, coming face-to-face with Larry, who was only inches from the door; so close to freedom.

Her calloused finger stopped at Larry's face, pointing directly at his nose. Larry swallowed and leaned backward against the wall as she began the slow build of a threatening speech. "Now you listen to me, Larry," she hissed, keeping the same close distance as the boy tried to drift away from her. "I'm watching your every move. If you're not back when the streetlights go on tonight, this will be the first and last day you leave the house for the rest of the year. I'll tie you to the bannister if I have to. Do you understand me?"

By now, Larry was pressed against the kitchen door. His wide eyes gave nothing away as his hands fumbled with the door latch. He saw his mum's arms coiled as if to grab him and he flipped the door open just in time to launch himself out of the house and avoid her grip. He scrambled down the side stairs into the cold morning air. Helen stood in the doorway, hands on her hips, watching him dash back away with a fire in her eyes.

"I'm watching you Larry!" she called after him as he turned and trotted briskly toward the park.

He only got four houses away before another voice called out his name. "Larry! Larry!" It was Ronnie Vautour, the kid Larry got on with best at the park. He was grinning ear to ear, talking a mile-a-minute and loud as ever. "Larry!" he shouted. "How about that fire last night huh? Can you believe the size of it? I think we scorched the damn benches …"

"Shh!" Larry said, finger at his lips, looking back at the distant doorway where his mum was still watching … always watching. Ronnie didn't stop talking. "I mean seriously Larry, that was a shocker and we even pulled the alarms, huh, what a blast!"

By now the two boys were close enough for Larry to reach out and smack Ronnie upside the head. "Shut up!" he said. Ronnie put his hand up to block the hit, while Larry looked over his shoulder, expecting his mum to be closing in on him at a sprint. Ronnie's eyes scanned the area as well. He lowered his voice.

"Sorry pal, I didn't realize this was spy stuff," he joked. "Next time we start a bonfire or something we'll do some kind of secret handshake not to say nothin', okay?"

Larry moved to slap him upside the head again. "I said shut up. Mum's on to me."

Ronnie laughed. "She's always on to you, pal. You can't sneeze without that woman throwing a shoe your direction. I don't know how she does it. She must have informants."

"Yeah, like you," Larry shot back.

"Me? Never!" Ronnie grinned. "Your secrets are safe with me. I'll never sell you out."

"No, but you'd shout about it all over the neighborhood," Larry grumbled, finally starting to relax. If she were going to do anything, she would have done it already. Larry offered the hard-boiled egg he snagged to Ronnie.

"Thanks, but no thanks. I had breakfast," Ronnie said as Larry took a bite. Another plane roared low overhead, its jet stream trailed behind like a deafening daylight comet. Ronnie waited for the din to die down before he reached into his pocket.

"But guess what? I got the goods," Ronnie said, pulling out two familiar coupons. "Lookie! Lookie! Bruins game time!" They were two buck-a-ticket coupons to the Bruins game. The slips got each boy a free seat on the upper level of the Garden. All they needed was a dollar for the bus and the train to get there. Larry's face lit up. The whole gang would be there, or at least everyone who could afford it.

"Who they playing?" He asked.

"It's New Year's Day, Larry! The Rangers," Ronnie started, going into detail about the recent history of this holiday showdown between the Bruins and the New York Rangers. "What was it ... two years ago the B's smashed them 6-0, can you believe that? Last year it was a tie 4-4. So this could be a screamer, Larry. This could be a big one. And no matter what, there'll be real fights, right?"

Larry smiled and slapped Ronnie on the back. "Atta kid!" The boys laughed but then Larry dropped his hands into his pockets, remembering the buck he needed to get into the city. "You got any dough?" Larry asked.

"Nah," said Ronnie. "I spent it all at the movies over Christmas. Did you see Man in the Saddle yet?" Larry shook his head. Westerns were his favorite when he did get a chance to go. Ronnie could see Larry's disappointment and kept talking: "Good, don't. It's crap anyway. Waste of money. It's got that Randolph Scott guy who's awful. No John Wayne means no movie is what I say. Say, you got any money now?"

"Nope," said Larry. "I left in a hurry this morning, what I got's in my room, and I don't think it's anywhere near two bucks." The two looked at each other in a panic. They were so close to seeing the game. It was just money in the way.

Ronnie kicked the ground and spoke up with resolve. "You know what, we'll get the money. No problem." Larry remembered Clara and Ruthie.

"Let's go down to the store. Clara's working today and she'll have something for us," The boys sometimes worked odd jobs at the store to make cash. If not there, then Nicky Aiosa could always set them up with a grocery delivery, which meant they got tips.

Larry and Ronnie were just seven, but they were only an afternoon of hustling away from seeing the Bruins play, all on their own. There was no snow on the ground yet so they couldn't get out the sleds to go coasting anyway. They pushed their hands into their pockets and walked toward the store. The days were always like this. Life went moment to moment. You never knew what was coming next, but you were always willing to play the game.

Carroll Cut-Rate was the place to go for a deal in Everett Square. It was part pharmacy, part thrift shop, and all at low prices. The back wall was lined with shelves and cases. Hopefully the back room was a mess so that Larry and Ronnie could make some money helping clean it up. They pushed open the shop door to the familiar sound of a tiny bell clattering against the doorframe. Clara was at the counter with Ruthie, reading magazines borrowed off a nearby shelf. Clara's blond hair flowed loose around her head, with one ribbon on top. Her coat was still on because the store was chilly.

"Good morning, gentlemen," Clara smiled as the two boys shook off the cold and peeked around, "how may I help you?" She watched her mother's young charge study the shelves before peering into the back room. He didn't even need to say anything for her to know what he was after. Clara was 19 and knew a thing or two about kids in search of cash. She liked Larry though, and she was going to enjoy hearing his angle this time. Plus, when there was work to be done in the store, he was good for it. He might have been a skinny little kid, but he always got the job done no matter how long it took.

"Say Clara," Larry said, cocking his head toward the back room, "you got any boxes that need stacking?" He reached to open the storage area door but Clara stopped him.

"Sorry, Larry. Ruthie and I took care of that this morning."

Ruthie looked up from her magazine long enough to wink at Larry, saying: "Guess you slept in too late." Larry frowned and bunched his hands in his pockets. Clara watched him pace the aisles a little more, his eyes on Ruthie as he walked. Larry and Ruthie were the same age, but Ruthie had a mom living nearby. Larry didn't. For years, the two had shared a room in Mrs. Giordano's house, and they used to always play together in the yard. Then they got their own rooms, and they started spending more time apart. They still walked to school together every morning, but things were different.

It changed when Ruthie's social worker came for her the first time a while ago. That time, Larry sat alone in the front yard and waited for her to come back. Helen called him in when the streetlights went on. This last week was the second time Ruthie had gone away. Larry made a point to stay in the park with the gang the whole time. He couldn't bring himself to wait around for her anymore.

Clara watched over him, knowing no matter what happened to Ruthie, Larry didn't have anyone coming to get him from the house, temporarily or not. Maybe that was a good thing though, she thought. Maybe staying at the house would keep Larry out of trouble. If he wasn't in trouble already, that is.

"You boys out late last night, by any chance?" she asked. The memory of flames and sirens from Swan Street Park jumped to everyone's minds at once.

Ronnie quickly changed the subject. "You think Mr. Aiosa needs any help?" he asked.

Clara shrugged and pointed to the door. "You can go ask him."

The boys looked at each other and decided to head out. "Bye Ruthie," Larry muttered, but the girl didn't acknowledge him. Clara watched the two boys shield their faces as they walked through the door and into the cold wind. The bell clanged suddenly as the door slammed behind them. Clara turned back to Ruthie.

"Larry's a good kid. What happened to you two?" she asked, "You used to be two peas in a pod." Ruthie started to speak, but couldn't think of what to say. Instead she flipped another page in the magazine. A smiling ad with a family packed into a blue Chevrolet stared up at her. Ruthie flipped another page and then pushed the magazine away.

Ruthie was silent. She didn't feel like Clara could understand. She didn't feel like anyone could understand. When Larry was a baby, his mother had left him. Larry didn't even know what her face looked like. Ruthie had just gotten back from Christmas with her mom, and it hadn't worked out again. She had been taken back to Helen's house again; left again, for the third time.

"You mad he got the bigger room?" Clara asked. Ruthie scanned the shelves around her and felt lost, but she made eye contact with Clara, and thought about how this tall blond girl was the closest thing to a sister she had. And that helped her speak up.

"You know something Clara?" she whispered, "I don't stay anywhere long enough to care how big my room is."

Then she pulled the magazine back and turned it to another page. She rested her head in her hand, covering the half of her face toward Clara, and lost herself in the newsprint. For a moment, Clara wondered how a girl so young could be so sad. She wondered how her own mother could manage it, taking in these foster kids. It seemed impossible that their house on Dean Street was big enough to hold them, along with her and her brothers when they came to visit. She looked out the window to see Larry in the distance pushing through the chill toward Everett Square. "I wonder what they're up to?" she wondered out loud. Ruthie didn't answer.

Larry and Ronnie pushed through another shop door. Working for Mr. Aiosa meant deliveries if he had any, and that was a long walk in the cold instead of being inside with Clara and Ruthie. But, if that was where the money was, they knew they were going for it.

Montello's Market was on Main Street. The boys ducked in as the January winds picked up. Mr. Aiosa, a thin man with glasses and kind eyes, was stocking shelves. "You need any help with deliveries today, sir?" Larry asked.

"Sure kid, pull your truck around back," the grocer joked. "We'll load it all up for you."

"Mr. Aiosa, why don't you let us stock these shelves for you?" Ronnie suggested, seeing a few open boxes on the floor next to the row of cold cases on the back wall.

"Sure thing, boys. Standard pay though. Nickel each."

The boys glanced at each other helplessly. Without speaking, they agreed that they might as well do this until they could think of something better to make up the rest. The store owner saw they were after more and leaned in closer.

"How much do you two need anyway?" he asked.

Ronnie stepped back and Larry bristled. Neither boy wanted to take charity. The slightest hint of it set off alarm bells in their head.

"Need?" Ronnie gasped incredulously. "Why, Mr. Aiosa, we're just offering to help out, right. Fair pay for fair work."

"Then it's a nickel each for those boxes. If I get a call for a delivery, I'll let you know."

With that, Larry and Ronnie got down to business, carefully placing each new can and carton behind the older products at the back of the shelves the way they had been taught to dozens of times before. It was semi-useless because the ladies who came in to do the shopping knew to reach back and grab the new shipments anyway. Some of the cans at the front of these shelves must have been years old.

As they neared the end of the boxes, the phone rang. "Hey guys, this might be an order," Mr. Aiosa smiled. He answered the phone and got out a pen to started writing. Ronnie spun to face Larry and silently mouthed, "Hot damn." Larry watched Mr. Aiosa intently, hoping the order was big enough that two boys carrying it across town would be worth two dollars to someone. The call ended too soon. Mr. Aiosa ripped the slip of paper off his pad and waved it toward them.

"Half-dozen eggs, quart of milk, and a box of biscuits. Delivery to Baker Road," Mr. Aiosa said. "Ten cents from me, plus whatever they tip you. You want it?"

Baker Road wasn't that far away. It wasn't nearly enough money either. But it was worth something. Larry and Ronnie nodded their agreement. They packed the box silently, filling it with the groceries and some papers to keep things from sliding around. Then Mr. Aiosa dropped the box in a bag as Larry and Ronnie prepared for another walk through the cold. "Go quick and come back to warm up, boys," Mr. Aiosa called after them, smiling. "And this is on her tab, so don't try taking any more money from her!"

The entire city of Everett is three square miles. It would fit easily in New York's Central Park. Inside those three square miles lived 46,000 people; every square foot of land would have three people on it if everyone were spread out evenly. And, there were two nine-year-old boys carrying a box of groceries through those crowded streets in the hope of making a dollar and ninety cents in tips for a New Year's Day grocery delivery. Ronnie knew that was never going to happen.

"Hold on Larry, let's stop by my house first," Ronnie said, indicating a left turn back to the neighborhood.

"What for?" Larry asked.

"Need a little back-up," the other boy said, winking.

So they changed direction and walked back up to Ronnie's house. Larry knew Ronnie's dad was with the fire department and had a great house painting business on the side. The family was doing all right. Still, he couldn't imagine there were dollar bills just lying around in there. Ronnie's mom, Peggy, was putting away Christmas decorations when they came in.

"Hi hon," she said to Ronnie. "Hi Larry," she smiled. "Is it cold out there, boys?"

"Sure is, Ma," Ronnie said, heading for the stairs. Larry lingered in the hallway, holding the groceries carefully. Peggy looked up for a moment.

"You need an extra layer, Larry?" she asked. "We've got one of Donnie's old coats." Donnie was one of Ronnie's four older brothers; a really big guy, who still stopped by the park from time to time. They might see him at the game tonight if they could get there.

"Thanks Mrs. Vautour," Larry said in a tone she found quietly familiar. "I'm all right."

This kid doesn't take anything from anyone, she thought.

"Nonsense," she said, and she dropped a heavy coat over his shoulders. "Leave it with Ronnie when you're done today," she said. The grocery bag caught her eye. "You two doing a delivery for Mr. Aiosa today?"

"Yes, ma'am," Larry said.

"On New Year's Day?"

"Yes, ma'am."

"Want someone to drive you?"

"No, ma'am, we can do it. It's not far at all. Baker Road."

Peggy wrapped packing paper around one of the shepherds in her porcelain nativity scene and placed it carefully in a box labeled "Creche."

"So what are you making for that delivery?" she asked Larry.

"A dime so far," Larry said.

She wrapped a wise man up and placed him in the same box.

"Good for you two," she said, nodding with approval. Ronnie ran down the stairs quickly, heading for the front door.

"Enough with the questions, Ma, we got work to do, okay?" he said, opening the door and practically pushing Larry outside. Peggy took a step into the doorway as the boys left.

"Don't you be short with me, Ronnie, you're the one who came out of your way for a Baker Road delivery. Why'd you come here, anyway?"

Ronnie held up his hands, now covered in thick knit wool.

"Gloves, Ma!" he said reaching into his pocket and tossing a pair to Larry. "Geez, we come for one second and we're on trial. Can we go already?" Peggy smiled and closed the door. They're good kids—good, good kids, she thought as she spread out two more sheets of paper to wrap up the delicate porcelain Mary.

Outside, Larry looked at the gloves and then looked back at Ronnie and asked, "What was that for? I don't need gloves." But Ronnie shushed him, darting off the sidewalk and into the bushes at the side of his house. He reached into the center of some thick branches and retrieved his prized possession: a Louisville Slugger baseball bat.

Ronnie rested the bat on his shoulder and sauntered toward Larry. He patted his pal on the shoulder and sighed. "Larry, Larry, Larry. We could get all the eggs in Boston to our fine customer in a matter of seconds and she still isn't tipping us an entire dollar for the bus. Okay?"

Larry nodded.

Ronnie gave the bat a light swing. "So this bat, my friend, is our ticket to the game. Trust me. C'mon."

The bus stopped at Everett Station, where a crowd of Bruins fans filed up the stairs onto the platform of the elevated train that took them to Boston Garden. Larry and Ronnie met up with Ronnie's brother Donnie and several other boys all brandishing their ticket coupons, all charged up to see the action on the ice. The station was alive with hockey talk. Opinions flew through the air about the Bruins' chances at the playoffs. Once again, things weren't going well. The Detroit Red Wings had run away with the league for three years in a row. The last time the Bruins gave them a run for their money was 1949. The train arrived and everyone piled in, ready to get to their seats.

This game had a lot behind it, and you could tell from the passengers. The Bruins were taking on the New York Rangers, a team they knew how to beat, but they didn't always get the job done. Guys on the train threw players' names around. It was a revenge match, coming after the Rangers put six past Bruins goalkeeper Jim Henry during an away game in December. The fans wanted to know if veteran Bruins center Milt Schmidt could pull through. The old guys were curious about the Rangers' new striker Wally Hergesheimer, who started out the season on a scoring streak.

Larry also heard the boys talking about the Rangers' Don Raleigh, who scored twice in overtime during the 1950 playoffs against the Red Wings. He weighed in at 150 pounds, earning him the nickname "Bones." Larry knew he could be the fastest kid at the park, even if he wasn't one of the biggest. So the idea of a little guy stacking up against the giants of all-pro hockey sounded pretty good. He thought about trying to get Bones' autograph after the game when the players filed out of the Garden.

Impatiently waiting for the train to Boston, Ronnie and Larry scanned the sea of coats and hats. Each guy had a grin on his face. They guffawed and slapped each other on the back as they imagined the clatter of body checks against the boards, thrown gloves, bloody noses, and the blaring buzzer keeping time with the periods. He and Ronnie stayed close to the older boys, finally shuffling into the train car surrounded by the camaraderie of the game, the mass of the crowd moved together as if to say: *No matter where we live, what we've done, or what the future brings, tonight we are going to see the Bruins.*

Ronnie and Larry looked at each other—heads high, chins up—one of the guys. They earned this. The loose change from the parking meters weighed in their pockets, but it couldn't distract from the reverberating laughter in the train car as more passengers joined them from Sullivan Station, Thompson Square, City Square, and finally the doors opened off Causeway Street.

It was a familiar drill for everyone. The ticket takers, older fans, and kids came together like family for a holiday tradition. The boys pulled out their coupons for the ticket takers snatch away and point to the doors leading up to the top landing. "Run as fast as you can boys, run!" they said. And like a staggered footrace, they took off. Larry and Ronnie leapt up the grimy cement stairs, busting through the double doors at the top level. Once inside, they weren't distracted by the gigantic black-and-yellow spoked B at center ice, or the team banners hanging from the ceiling. They raced *en masse* with sneakers pounding against each other and arms guarding their space in the pack all the way to the first row of the first balcony where they dropped down, took a seat on the front stair, and leaned over to admire the rink beneath them. The red lines and blue circles were laid out in vivid detail. With their place secure, they elbowed each other with glee.

Larry scanned the doors around the Garden as fans streamed in to join them. This morning, he had been up against the wall in the kitchen facing the wrath of Mrs. Giordano. Now, just a few hours later, he was in the beating heart of Boston, surrounded by the guys. He belonged here, and he felt it in his heart as the chaos and the noise of a filled arena pounded in his ears. Seven years old and the city belonged to him. All he had to do was pound it out of a few parking meters, and here he was.

Echoes of curses and jeers reached the kids' ears from every corner. The odd Rangers fan was shouldered in line for beer. The vendors came through selling nuts and pretzels. Donnie laughed as his younger brother bought him a bag of nuts. Larry shelled out for pretzels for the group. The older boy knew better than to ask where they got the cash. Instead, he clapped each of them on the shoulder and they ate and watched the players clamber out onto the ice for the warm-up. *What's mine is yours, what's yours is mine* was always the ethos of the Swan Street Rats. They lived by it on the baseball diamond, on the streets beside their homes, and here surrounded by the sights, smells, and swelling crowds in the city. Nobody had to say it, but if you had something, the group had it. The buzzer rang to start the first period. It was so loud Larry and Ronnie could feel it in their stomachs.

The puck hit the ice and the Rats had their rightful place above it all in the balcony at the Garden, which had a name, by the way. Larry wasn't surprised to hear it the first time he came to a game. Their seats were in the part of the arena called *The Heavens*.

After a bruising three periods, the Bruins fell to the Rangers 4 to 2. But the score line didn't matter much after the excitement of it all. The fans stood, shouted, cursed, and kicked the floor. Larry and Ronnie joined in, looking left to right and picking their favorite comments to repeat as the players slid off the ice. They may have lost again, but they were the Bruins.

"That's our team, Larry," Ronnie laughed. "They lost by two goals but they fought like hell."

Donnie leaned down to elaborate. "Six teams in the league, five will beat you and one will break your nose. That's us, boys."

The arena lights were on full force now, and the top level was emptying out slowly. Donnie nodded to the west side of the Garden. "We gonna go try for autographs?"

Larry knew his chances of making it home in time for his mum's curfew were almost gone already. The 20-minute train ride and 5-minute bus ride could get him to Dean Street in time, if he was lucky. But he didn't want this time at the game to end. He was with Donnie, Ronnie, and the rest of the gang. "Let's do it," he said.

His mum's anger would be temporary. An autograph would be forever. In the familiar world of Swan Street Park, there were kids with new bikes and gloves. There were kids who got a new coat every year and had more than one pair of shoes. But there were damn few who had an autographed Bruins program. Donnie led them to the side lot, along with the core group of Everett kids. They elbowed their way to the front of the line. Larry and Ronnie slipped through the small spaces between waving fans. This was the place where kids from all over stood and shouted at their heroes as they left the game and loaded up on the team buses. It didn't matter what team they were on. These were pro hockey players. Everything they did would be remembered forever, no matter how loudly they were booed on the ice.

Larry shouted with the rest as each big, tired man waved and trudged past. He pushed out his program, but other fans snapped up the few players who stopped. A guy right next to him got a photograph signed. Larry watched it happen. Ronnie smiled and raised his eyebrows: "Maybe we're next."

No such luck. Big Ed Sandford, the Bruins winger, stopped

signing before he reached them and moved for the bus. The other players didn't sign at all. "Ah, c'mon," Donnie complained, but the bus doors shut. "Well, next time huh?"

Larry saw a nearby boy waving his autograph around emphatically and considered decking him to take it. Ronnie elbowed him in the shoulder. "Next time, Larry, c'mon. Let's go home."

On the way home, the boys relived the best moments of the game. Their pack walked up Broadway together, greeting shop owners and guys on the street, slowly breaking up as each Swan Street Rat split off for home. By the time Dean Street came up, Larry was resigned to a walloping from his mum.

Ronnie looked him. "Is it going to go rough for you in there?" he asked.

"We'll see," Larry said, brushing it off. "I'll be fine."

"Sure you will," Ronnie said. "See you tomorrow."

Larry turned to the familiar dark stairway through the side porch door. The same feelings as last night washed over him. *Would she be waiting for him? Or, more precisely, where would she be waiting?* he thought. For a moment, he wondered why she would wait for him. Why? Why was she doing this to him? Helen Giordano wasn't his real mother. Wouldn't it be easier for her if she just left him alone? He'd been through enough already. He had nothing—no mother, no father, no sister, no brothers—and now not even an autograph. Maybe she could let him get away with it just this once. It wasn't too much to ask.

He took a first step up the stairs, then another and another. The hair on the back of his neck stood up and his fingers tingled the closer he got to the door at the top. If it was locked, he was done for. She would come up the stairs for him. He had delivered groceries, busted parking meters, run from a cop, gone to a Bruins game, and came home all right and … the idea of his mum catching him struck the fear of God into him.

But he'd be damned if he was going to show it.

He stiffened his lip and reached for the handle. The door was locked. Behind him, the growing shadow of his foster mother filled the stairway. Game over.

❖ ❖ ❖

A young person's mind is special. Some people say it's like a sponge, that it soaks up the world around it, changing who that boy or girl grows up to be. Some people say it's a lump of clay, being sculpted and molded by events. In that moment, Larry's mind was a race car spinning its wheels. His eyes were fixed on Mrs. Giordano, who was moving slowly, one step at a time, broom in hand, eyes flashing with the fires of retribution. Whatever was coming, Larry would need a miracle to escape.

"Where have you been?" Mrs. Giordano seethed. The chilled air showed the steam of her breath. Only four steps away now. Her hands were reaching out.

Larry shifted to the side and pushed his back to the wall to try and slip down the stairs. She was ready. Her goaltending was flawless as she body-checked his escape attempt and grabbed him by the nearest vulnerable ear. The familiar vice grip stopped Larry instantly. Thrashing was useless. Instead he tried to kick out with his left leg. The only result was the clinking of change shifting in his pockets. Helen's already-enraged eyes widened. She looked down at his pockets.

"What's that sound?" She asked.

"Just some change," Larry said. Hoping for some way out, any escape would do.

"And where did you get it?" She demanded, the broomstick jutting toward Larry's eyes.

"We made a delivery for the store. It was a tip," Larry lied carefully, trying to tell enough of the truth to convince himself. But his mum was no pushover. She pulled him down the stairs and into the soft light of the living room lamp, making it easier to observe Larry's panicked eyes.

"Empty those pockets," she commanded.

"It's nothing, really."

"*I said empty them.*"

Larry gulped and slowly reached into his right pocket. Out came the ticket stub from the game. Helen looked it over. "That explains why you're late, but where'd the money come from? *Empty them.*"

Larry reached back in and pulled out as much change as he could fit into one fist, dropping it carefully onto the walnut side table. Nickels spread out over the surface. Helen tapped the pocket and heard more rattling. "All of it," she demanded.

Larry put both hands in his pockets and pulled out two more

fistfuls. She watched him reach back in and pull another fistful out. The side table held a mound of coins beyond anything Larry could have possibly earned honestly. "That's an awful lot of nickels, boy," she hissed. "Turn those pockets inside out."

He slowly complied, and another few nickels fell to the floor. One rolled off into the dining room, spinning to a stop on the hardwood floor. The sound of it clattering awakened all the fears Helen has for this boy in her care, reverberating through her head as if it were the sound of a prison door slamming shut. She took a deep breath and centered herself as if to say, *The line will be drawn here*. He would not go to that place. She walked to her chair, sat back, and turned the lamp to shine on the boy.

His eyes went from the pile of money to his foster mother and back. In that moment, he was helpless to deny it. It was impossible to pretend that this situation was all right. But he was never, ever going to admit anything. And he didn't have to. She spoke for him.

"You couldn't afford the bus so you stole money, didn't you, Larry?" She asked.

Larry refused to answer. The two stared each other down. In that moment, they both realized the strength they were facing. Larry saw the one person he feared, the one person he didn't want to anger, and, looking at her eyes, searching his for answers … he felt like she was the one person he didn't want to disappoint. But he had, and he couldn't bring himself to be sorry for a second. He stared back at the woman who was his whole family and smirked, as if to say, *Whatever you're going to do to me, get on with it*.

Helen saw him, and she saw a boy walking the edge between two lives. On one side, whatever he stole today was just the beginning. He was falling away from her toward a life she wanted to protect him from. She wanted him to know that he would have a better future if he stayed out of trouble now She didn't want to live her waking nightmare of Larry in handcuffs. Larry calling her from the station. Larry being lost to her because she failed him.

Strength was the answer, she thought. *I will not let him live like this*.

The next morning, Helen's neighbor, Louise, looked out her kitchen window the way she normally did before cooking breakfast—carefully inspecting the neighborhood for any new gossip. She saw something that shocked her to complete attention. The iron railing around Mrs. Giordano's porch had something wrapped around it. She peered closer and saw two sneakers stretched out on the porch. There was a rope trailing from the railing to … was it?

Yes, it was. It was a boy!

Louise rushed out her front door, apron trailing behind her. She flew up the stairs to find Larry coiled in a rope and tied up to the porch railing. She stopped in horror, calling out, "Are you okay?"

Larry shrugged.

Mrs. Giordano opened the door behind Louise, bringing out a plate of toast, a bowl of oatmeal, and a glass of water on a tray. "Here's your breakfast. Eat up," she said to Larry, dropping the tray on his lap.

Louise stared in disbelief. "Helen, what is this?" she gasped.

Helen turned and headed back inside, stating matter-of-factly over her shoulder: "He got into trouble yesterday, so I'm keeping him on a short leash."

After breakfast, Mrs. Giordano moved Larry inside, but kept him tied tight. His back arched against the stairway banister as Ruthie and her friends raced up and down the stairs. They didn't stop to question why he was there. It was just another simple fact of life. If you crossed Mum, you could end up roped to the stairs. There was no need to think about it beyond that. Plus, the woman of the house walked by her prisoner frequently, keeping visitors away. Sometimes Helen even dusted the landing around him like he was another knick knack on a shelf.

Larry's stiff upper lip only got stiffer. He was not sure of much in this world, but he was sure that he was never, ever going to give in. And that was when Benny walked into the house.

Mrs. Giordano's son, Benny Giordano, was a big guy, both physically and in the eyes of all the kids in the house. His broad, square shoulders and easy smile brought the kids to him from every corner of the house. Ruthie ran up and gave him a big hug.

"Benny! You here for long?" she called out, falling into his arms.

"Just for the day, Ruthie," Benny grinned, patting the others on the head. "Ma called me up to say hello."

Benny had graduated from Boston College. He had been on the football team. His name appeared in the stat sheets and the guys used to talk about him all over town. He also played baseball in the park and had a mean swing that sent more than a few balls through windows.

Larry sat up straight and watched him talking to the kids. Ruthie slipped back upstairs, shaking her head at Larry's ropes on the way up. Suddenly feeling self-conscious, Larry tried to act like he had chosen to sit at the base of the stairs on his own. He crossed his arms over some of the rope knots and acted natural. Benny half-smirked at him before striding over to the kitchen to talk to his mom. Larry strained to hear what they were saying, but with no luck. The muffled voices in the kitchen stopped. There was a long pause and Benny came out and stopped to talk to Larry for the first time. He grinned again at the younger boy. Larry couldn't help but grin sheepishly back. "Hittin' parkin' meters, are ya?" Benny questioned.

The smile fell off Larry's face. Suspicion returned and he peered around, looking for his mum's prying ears. Benny grabbed a dining room chair and swung it effortlessly over his shoulder, dropping it with a deep clunk next to Larry and sitting down beside him. The two looked at each other. Benny shook his head.

"She's not stupid, Larry. She knows how a kid your age gets a pocket full of change," he said. "But you're whackin' them earlier than some of us got to it. How many did you take?"

Larry's eyes brightened at the hint of a compliment. He slowly raised his hand and extended four fingers, a count that didn't include his failed first swing. Benny whistled. "Four, huh? Not bad, kid. Anyone see you?"

Larry's eyes lowered again. He would have liked to brag about outrunning Vinnie Amigo the motorcycle cop, but he wasn't about to be stupid talking Benny, someone who would definitely report back to his mum.

"I'm serious," Benny insisted. "Did you get away clean?"

"Clean enough," Larry said, shrugging. "Until this," he added, gesturing to the ropes.

"Sure, sure," Benny said; the ropes didn't seem too bad to him. Larry guessed he must have gotten the same treatment growing up. In a way it made Larry feel good, like he was part of the family. Benny continued: "Why'd you do it, anyway? Candy money?"

Larry shook his head. "We went to the Bruins game, Benny," he whispered excitedly. "And you won't believe it, I was this close to getting an autograph after." Larry's immobilized arms came together to indicate a couple of inches of space between his hands.

"Is that so?" Benny wondered. "Who from?"

"I was hoping for Don Raleigh," Larry said, remembering the little guy who scored big goals for the Rangers.

"You mean Bones?" Benny chuckled. "What about some of the hometown guys?"

"Ed Sanford was right there, but he signed something for another kid and got on the bus," Larry grumbled.

"Is that why you got home so late?" Benny wondered.

Larry nodded. "Guess she told you all about it, huh?" he sighed. "Even about the side door steps."

Benny chuckled again. "You aren't the only one to have been caught on those steps."

Larry looked up, his eyes scanning Benny's face. He was looking for some kind of approval—a sign that getting a smack now and again was all right—a sign that it was fine to take what you wanted, because nobody was looking out for you but yourself and the rest of the gang.

He was looking for something that said, "Sure, you got in trouble, but 'atta boy."

But that was not there. Benny's eyes said something else—something Larry wasn't used to. He couldn't figure out what it was.

"Look, kid," Benny said. "You are *family* to me, okay?" Larry's eyes widened. "And I'm like your older brother in this house."

Larry sat up at attention as Benny continued.

"I've been in Everett my whole life. There's nothing, and you look at me ... believe me ... when I say that there is *nothing* you are going to do on these streets that I haven't done before. My brother did it before me." Larry listened.

"You go down to the park. We went down to the park. You go down to the pool hall. We went down to the pool hall. You chase girls—when you get to that—and guess what? We chased girls all over this town. Do ya get it?"

Larry looked sideways grinning at the thought. Benny got off the chair and crouched closer to Larry. "Listen to me, Larry. Listen good," he said, pointing to the kitchen where Helen was cooking. "That woman in there, she's all you got. She's my mother and I know her. I can tell she wants the best for you. But it's up to you to be smart. Keep out of trouble. Because she's there for you and

35

someday you'll know what that means the way I know what it means. And I'm telling you, it means a whole hell of a lot."

Larry listened. He tried to make sense of what Benny was saying. In the end, he just nodded. Benny stood up, patted the boy on the head, and lifted the chair lightly back into place in the dining room. Helen gave Benny a knowing look that Larry didn't understand. The two went into the kitchen together. There was more low talking.

Still tied to the bannister, Larry felt a sense of wonder. He scanned the room with new eyes. It couldn't be put into words, but his heart had a sense of something important. It was as if he knew that he had been a troublemaker, but now he knew that he was part of a long line of troublemakers. He knew that Benny and his mum wanted him to be part of their family. Larry, stuck at the base of her stairs, felt like he belonged.

Helen untied Larry after Benny left. She gave him chores to do all day, eyeing him suspiciously so he knew he was being watched more closely than ever. Over the next couple of days, he smiled more than he had in months. When he could finally to go to the park, he came home on time. He ate with the other kids in the house and there was a new harmony that lasted for days.

Larry was still Larry, and his mischievous streak continued, but Helen saw something else in him. When he felt like he belonged, she thought, he stood a little taller. He had the attitude of a champion.

A week after the rope punishment, Larry came home from a cold day outside. His nose was red. His hands were buried deep in his pockets. He stamped his feet to warm up before entering the kitchen. "There's someone to here to see you, Larry," Helen said. "She's in the living room." Larry went cold. He knew what that meant.

Around the corner in the living room, a prim young woman sat upright in the floral chair where nobody ever sat. Her eyes passed over the room mechanically before her head turned toward Larry. Her eyes widened and her lips curled into a forced smile. Larry had visitors from the state. They were social workers. They came almost every month, with a notepad and a lot of questions.

"Hi there Larry, you remember me, don't you? I'm Miss Power," she cooed. Larry tried not to roll his eyes. He shuffled into the room and sunk into the couch cushions across from the chair. He tried to disappear while she launched into more sweet-sounding words that he didn't really understand. All he knew was that someone like this came for Ruthie every time she was taken away. He didn't care what she said as long as she left, soon, without him.

"Helen tells me you're doing just fine and that you've become quite the little man," she said. "Did you have a good Christmas?"

"Ya, it was fine," Larry said.

"Are you staying out of trouble?" she asked.

Larry thought back to the Christmas trees burning in the park, the way the baseball bat had felt bashing into each parking meter. He thought about his escape from Vinnie Amigo the motorcycle cop with Ronnie and being tied to the stairway. "I'm never in trouble," he said.

"Good!" she said.

Larry watched her write something down in the pad. *What did she write down?* he thought. He imagined elaborate plans to take him away from his mum and the gang at the park. He wanted to stand up and shout at her, *You can't take me away!* But he sat quietly. It seemed that she was out of questions. School hadn't started back up yet so she couldn't ask about that. Usually that was all they talked about. *What did you do in school today? What is your favorite subject? Do you like your teacher?* He felt like saying if she wanted to know so bad she should go to school instead of him. She didn't matter anyway. In a month there would be a new one, asking the same questions. Finally, she stood up.

"Well, it was nice to see you, Larry," she said with another fake smile. For a moment it seemed as if she would pat him on the head, so he sunk further into the couch cushion. Instead, she spun around to leave. Helen came to the door to let her out and watched her step down the porch stairs to a car waiting at the curb. Larry looked at his mum. He wondered if she had told the agent about anything.

"I told her we love having you here in the house more than ever, Larry," she said. "You don't have to worry about leaving. I won't let that happen."

Larry stood up and shuffled over to her as the agent's car sped away. Her hand ran through his hair and she looked down at him.

"Something came for you today," she said, leading him into the kitchen where a big manila envelope was waiting. Larry looked up at her, confused about what it was.

"Benny left it for you," Helen said. Larry fumbled to open it, his hands shaking with excitement. He lifted the flap and slid out a big, glossy football team photo, with Benny at the center of the group grinning up at him. The slate in front read "1950 Boston College Eagles Football." There was a note with it. Larry's lips moved along in wonder as he read it carefully. "Hear you're doing good, kid. Here's a pic of some of the local boys. - Benny." The envelope was filled with Benny's BC football game programs, complete with stats on each player and more photos.

Larry spread it all out on the table in front of him. His heart beat stronger and faster than he thought possible. It meant more to him than a pro hockey player's signature. He stood up, took them to his room, and placed the programs on his dresser. He tacked the team photo to his wall.

As long as he lived there, Larry would never take that photo down.

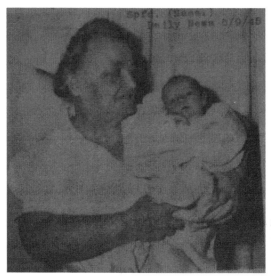

Larry after being found abandoned in the Kimball Hotel with a
nurse at the City Home in Springfield, Massachusetts

Larry at around age 3, when he was brought to live at Helen
Giordano's house in Everett, Massachusetts

Helen Giordano with her daughter, Clara, who lived at home
for part of the time her mother began cared for foster children

Ruthie and Larry (left) and Larry (right) in the yard at Helen
Giordano's house

Helen Giordano with Larry and Ruthie on the way to church

Two of Larry's photographs from the Devens School

Everett High School 1943 Team

Everett 21   Everett 19   Everett 7   Everett 6
Somerville 0   Salem 0   Medford 0   Waltham 7
Everett 35   Everett 7   Everett 13   Everett 30
Rindge 0   Lynn Class 0   Malden 0   Lynn Eng. 0

Benny Giordano (far left, #67) on the Everett High School
Football Team

The Boston College football team photo Benny Giordano gave to Larry, complete with a checkmark Larry drew on Benny's shoulder (second row from top, third from left)

Winter faded to spring and Larry's life drifted from braving frozen streets with hands in pockets to going where he truly belonged: the park. In warmer weather, Swan Street Park became the beating heart of the neighborhood. It filled with the rising sounds of kids playing, squeaking sneakers on the basketball court, grass-stained boys shouting like third-base coaches, and girls playing marbles on the sidewalk.

Every chance to slide into home was taken. Every home run was a full count, ninth inning, World Series shot over center field. Every play was a battle. The fights were real, but contained to their gang. The moment an outsider barged in on their territory, they united as one to push him out again, whether it was a kid from another gang down the line or an exasperated homeowner bordering the park calling for quiet or threatening to call the cops. This was the kids' home. The regulars—Larry, Ronnie, Paul Amici, Lou Fisk, Sonny Rocco, Joe Leo, Richie Eagan, Joey Medugno—all came down every day. The dirt on that park diamond dug under their nails and flowed through their blood. They'd play with the same equipment until it broke. When someone split a ball with a monster hit, they'd tape it up and keep playing. When it broke again, they'd go talk to Bobby Caramanica down at the Elm Street Rec Center to get more equipment, or they'd wait for Benny to come bring more bats and balls for them. If it rained, they would go down to the Rec Center and play hockey. If it was too hot, they could go to the Somerville pool or the Charlestown Boys and Girls Club. They could even hop the blue bus and go to Revere Beach. One time when they were bored, they took the subway as a group to Franklin Park Zoo, like one big dusty family.

And Larry grew into the core of it all, from a small kid taking orders, waiting for a chance to play, to a scrappy 10-year-old grabbing spots in the outfield and using his pace to turn infield drives into base hits. By the time he was 12, he had become heir to the Swan Street Rats leadership. He helped run the show, playing shortstop and first base, smashing glorious rainbows over the hill and back fence—occasionally hearing the musical tinkle of a broken window. Somehow it was still a pleasant sound, even though it meant he was facing a forced apology to the people in the house and money taken out of his piggy bank to pay for a new pane of glass.

As school wound down, the park days extended with the daylight in the afternoons and evenings. By summer they lasted all day, every day. The society run by the Swan Street Rats reigned over a dozen hours between breakfast and the hollers for dinner coming from porches around the park. The bright sun and cool mornings became grinding midday heat and then dark, muggy evenings. The deep pink and purple sunsets were criss-crossed by jet streams as planes landed and left. The world outside the park was ignored for the important work of playing endless sandlot games. It took a lot to stop them, for even a moment.

Old Man Parker was determined to stop them, though. He taught at the high school, but for whatever reason he didn't like the sound of kids. Unfortunately for him, his house sat on the nearest corner to Swan Street Park and the infinite yelling that accompanied endless baseball games.

Despite the fact that these kids virtually owned the park, Old Man Parker got fed up with the noise on a late summer day. Mr. Parker expressed himself by stepping out on his front lawn, clenching his heavy fists. He shouted toward the diamond cluttered with jockeying, bat-swinging, mini major leaguers, "Will you shut up!"

Larry looked over at Ronnie to share a familiar mischievous look. Different things happened next. First they all laughed and shouted back: "Take a hike!" "You shut up!" and a chorus of other gleeful backtalk. These responses came from the kids who were yet to sit in Mr. Parker's high school classes. Mr. Parker shot back with threats.

"You just wait until I talk to your parents," he responded. The yelling escalated until the enraged old man stormed inside, slamming his heavy blue front door like a thunderclap. Then Larry sprang into action with a plan. The rusty trash cans in the park usually had a couple of brown paper lunch sacks in them. He'd pull one out and empty it, then walk the park perimeter to find the largest dog turds available. Fortunately, there was never a shortage. The smaller kids followed along, giggling. They were wide-eyed, fascinated, and taking mental notes.

This is how the neighborhood worked. The rituals passed down from one kid to another. Now they were with Larry and he had learned his lessons well. Larry belonged in the park. And, no matter how many times callous adults leaning on fences or kids from across town called him a state ward, he knew in these moments that Larry Gagnon didn't need anyone else to give him respect. There were these moments where he took it himself. And at 12, he took that respect by showing Old Man Parker not to mess with his friends. He taught the teacher that he couldn't tell the Swan Street Rats what to do and when to shut up.

Ronnie lit the crap-filled bag on fire and Larry ran it to the base of that heavy blue door, rang the bell, and ran. The flames engulfed the entire bag before the door opened and the angry old man's eyes widened. Despite this having happened a dozen times before, the instinct to stamp out a fire on his porch was too great. His foot came down on the flaming bag, messing his shoe and the porch and setting off a wave of muffled laughter from a small army of kids carefully hidden in bushes, behind trees, and around corners all around. Larry and Ronnie celebrated with a professional handshake. The other kids looked on with admiration. The students had learned a valuable lesson: They learned that they could strike back.

Mischief was their best defense in a world of adults trying to tell Larry what to do. If someone came down to the park to yell at one of the Rats, he'd remember which house they came out of and wait until they put out a huge load of white laundry to dry before bringing a couple of the guys to cut their clotheslines.

They pushed that mischief to the very edge. A small crap fire on the porch was only the beginning. There were larger fires in trash cans and on park benches. The motorcycle cop Vinny Amigo rode into the park one too many times, so the gang ran a taut length of rope between the fence posts at the entryway. The next time he kicked his engine into gear and coasted into the park, the shocked officer was knocked off his ride with an unexpected blow to the chest.

Each moment of glorious mayhem disappeared in seconds, as the kids melted into individual yards and porches, protected by the sentiment from parents and other adults who sighed, "Boys will be boys" and "As long as he's home for dinner."

When he was very little, Larry never asked, "Why me?" As a 6-year-old running rampant through the three-decker houses of Everett, he was always aware that some kids had more stuff, but it didn't bother him. Over time, though, this attitude started to wear thin.

It was fun shopping at the discount store until he learned other kids went to department stores. It was fine to have his comfortable baseball glove, until he grew and all the other guys got new ones before he did. Walking home was okay until all the other kids zipped by on new bikes. Every new sneaker, every new baseball jersey, every shiny button on a new coat or fresh backpack for a new school year was beyond reach for Larry.

It wasn't long before each of those things on a passing kid made Larry feel a pang. It made him ask, "Why me?" and the question got louder and louder the older he got.

Helen did the best she could. The state's allotment for each foster kid amounted to $19 for clothes and a Christmas bonus that would cover a modest gift. The rest of the state support went toward food. She even had to ask in advance to get a social worker's permission to take one of the kids to a doctor, and she had to show a receipt afterward for the treatment or prescription. That meant that Larry's Sunday dress clothes for church; a new pair of sneakers; and a couple slacks, shirts, underwear, and socks ate up the yearly budget in the blink of an eye.

Unbeknownst to Helen, parking meters were smashed, groceries were delivered, and hustling was done for the rest of his needs: candy, doughnuts, and coffee for him and Ruthie and Clara; 25-cent movies on Saturday. The kids on their new bikes didn't get it, Larry thought. Everything he had was what he could put together for himself, or what the Swan Street Rats had stashed at each other's houses. (Later on, those stashes included some dirty magazines, the occasional six-pack of beer, and money to play pool in colder weather.) He and the guys pulled it together on their own. It became commonplace that if he wasn't going to be given something, he had to get it for himself. That's what happened with the bike when he was 11.

Eddie Carroll rode around on that bike like he owned the neighborhood. It had shiny chrome finishes around the wheels and pale blue paint on the body. He'd had it a couple days when Larry walked by Eddie's house to see him effortlessly drop the kickstand and dart inside for dinner. So Larry walked by again the next day. Same thing. The bike was in the same place under the garage overhang. The days after that featured additional sleuthing, and considering his options.

Eddie's dad must have told his son to be more careful, because the bike disappeared from view. Larry saw its new home was around back on the gravel by the hose. He hadn't decided to take it yet. But it was nice to know where it was, just in case he needed it. Or really wanted it. Sometimes it was hard to tell which was which.

In a place the size of Everett, a bike was like a time machine. With only three square miles, Larry could get from one side of the city to the other in minutes on a bike. Otherwise he was walking. Nothing was wrong with that, except on a bike the wind rushes through your hair and the houses pass by so quickly it feels like freedom. On foot, each step felt like another familiar refrain: "Why me?"

Larry made a decision to return to the back of Eddie's house.

Ronnie was down the street with some of the other guys when Larry rode up on the brand-new, shiny bike. "Look at that," Ronnie whistled. Gliding up to the guys, Larry felt something like relief. For once, he was the one with something turning heads. Maybe this meant they were jealous of him this time.

"Nice bike there, roostah," Billy Carrigan said, using Larry's nickname, and sauntering over to the bike the way grown men in the neighborhood did when someone pulled in with a new car. "Where'd ya get it?"

Larry didn't need to lie so much as tell the story he wished had happened, the story he felt like he deserved to tell: "Me and mum saved up. She took me down to get it this morning."

Ronnie circled it with a grin. He noticed that it was just like Eddie's, that kid from the other side of the neighborhood. But out loud he said, "All that saving paid off, Larry. Look at that."

The boys could see their grass-stained shorts in the chrome of Larry's new bike. He cut their appreciative chatter short to ride down to the store and show Ruthie and Clara. Ruthie looked at him and his big smile. She let her suspicion and jealousy slip away and gave him a big hug. Clara smiled too. "A lot of deliveries to get that, Larry," she said.

"It sure was," he said, and peddled off down the line and then over to the school. His hair brushed back in the breeze like an the feathers on an eagle chasing the horizon. His heart burst with a thousand feelings, and one of them was the desperation of knowing this couldn't last.

Meanwhile, Eddie's dad was showing a detective the bike's serial number and muttering about the state ward he had seen hanging out around the house. By nightfall, the detective was equipped with the names and addresses of foster homes in the city, and prepared to visit Helen Giordano's house.

That evening, Larry came home and carefully hid the bike around back. He treated it like a delicate work of art, covering it with an old tarp and secluding it near the bushes. He came in to dinner grinning inside and out. Ruthie smiled back, so did Clara. But neither of them brought it up. Somehow they knew, and they didn't want this moment of exhilaration to end for him. The entire meal felt as if Larry had pulled off a bank heist and his gang was playing it cool by passing the mashed potatoes instead of talking about the new bike.

"Did you have a good day, Larry?" Helen asked.

"Yeah, pretty good," Larry said. His mind flashed to the blur of houses and Billy's low, jealous whistle.

"You seem pleased with yourself," she added.

Larry stifled his grin and wondered if, as usual, his mum already knew what he'd been up to. Even though he had carefully placed the bike on a side of the house beyond view of the kitchen window, he didn't doubt her ability to see through solid walls. But she let it go.

"Good day for you, Ruthie?" she asked.

"It sure was, it was entertaining," Ruthie giggled.

"Was it?" Helen asked Clara.

"It always is down at the store," Clara said. "But today we had some cool customers." She winked at Larry. His grin returned.

The dinner meandered into plans for the family's visit to Helen's cabin in New Hampshire over the summer. Larry hated the idea of being separated from the guys, but he did like being on vacation. They could cannonball into the cool lake and go fishing,

49

too. Mostly he wondered if somehow he could sneak the bike up there with them. He imagined the trees whizzing by as he flew through the small, winding roads around the cabins. The dream was very much alive in him that night as he lay himself to sleep and in the morning as he ate breakfast. It didn't survive much longer, though, as the sound of knocks struck the front door and Helen looked out the window to see her worst fear. Detective O'Donnell was on her porch to ask Larry about some stolen property.

The detective stood solemnly. He had stopped by two other houses first, and confirmed the bike wasn't at either of them. The boy inside was the most likely to have taken it. As a police officer, he knew a lot about kids in foster homes. Sometimes he got calls about fighting in a house and it was a kid in the system trying to return home to a rough family. He'd taken a few kids back to foster parents. It was usually a relief to get them away from the shouting, but it was never a happy moment.

The foster mother would often wait near the door, knowing the child was going to come back. Her heart broke that the kid couldn't be with his or her real parents, but she was full of love and devotion. Although the detective had never heard a kid say to a foster mom, "I love you," he could see it. There were no tears of joy, the kind he saw when he found lost kids and brought them home to terrified parents; there were tears of relief. There was a feeling that this was where the kid was safe, and, for better or for worse, this was the adult who was really looking out for that child now.

The minute he knocked at Helen Giordano's house and saw the strong, clear-eyed, woman open the door and grow pale with fear at the sight of his badge, he knew what kind of mother she was. She had been working to stop this moment from happening. This was the look he saw in so many parents' faces when he came calling. He brought his hand up to his mouth, running the index finger and thumb to the corners of his lips, and gave a routine sigh.

"Sorry to bother you, ma'am," he said. His eyes gave nothing away, but he was thinking about how to make this easier on her and the boy inside. "I'm here to ask about a bike that's gone missing in the neighborhood. May I look around?"

Helen nodded silently and turned to show him through the house. Along the way, she pulled Larry to her side. The other kids were silent. Ruthie watched the officer, her mum, and Larry go outside with a forlorn stare. It was almost exactly what she suspected would happen when Larry rode up on that bike, but it was more frightening than she expected.

The small yard wasn't difficult to search. It took only a couple of glances to notice the bike-shaped tarp behind a bush. Larry barely reacted, his head cast aside, as the bike was unveiled in a grave singular motion. Still, the detective drew no conclusions. He fished a sheet of paper with the serial number out of his pocket. Then he found the exact corresponding numbers on the crossbar beneath the brand-new handles. He pushed the paper back into his pocket with a sense of finality. Case closed. But looking over at Helen and Larry, he knew finding the bike was the easy part of his job.

He straightened up to full stature and walked over to the boy and his mum. His hand rested on his hip and he nodded over at the bike. "That's the bike I'm looking for alright. The serial number matches," he stated, and looked down at Larry to clue him in, just in case his wheels were turning on a future attempt. "And even if that serial number weren't there for some reason, there are ways of knowing if it's a stolen bike. Any idea how it got under a tarp in your yard, son?"

Larry didn't look up. He shook his head.

"Well, I've got a pretty good idea," the detective continued. "I got an idea that you saw a bike you liked and waited for the right time to grab it, then you hid it there. Is that what happened?"

Larry shrugged.

"I think it is," the detective concluded.

Larry looked up. He knew he'd been caught and that he was wrong, but he also knew this cop didn't walk around every day wondering, *Why me?* The detective didn't see everyone else getting things while he didn't even get a hug from his father at Christmas, or a grandparent to visit.

Larry had got only his mum. He knew he'd let her down by grabbing the bike, and that he would never be able to make this up to her. It was the worst feeling in the world. So he looked at the detective with a still and featureless expression, like the lid of a teapot that doesn't change color or shape despite the boiling water it holds inside.

"What's your name, son?" the detective asked.

"Larry."

The detective pulled out his pen and pad. "Last name?"

"Gagnon."

"Okay, Larry Gagnon. And this is your foster mother, right?"

"She's my mum," Larry said.

"She does her best to take care of you, doesn't she?"

Larry nodded. He couldn't look up at her, but he could feel her watchful gaze on his shoulders. The weight increased with every word from the cop.

"Listen to me, son. I've written your name down here. Here is what that means. Me and the other boys down at the station have your name as a person we are going to watch." The detective pointed to his own eyes and then to Larry. Then he continued.

"That means if something goes missing around here, or if something happens in this neighborhood and we get called, we're going to flip through our notes down at the station and your name is going to come up, and we're going to say to ourselves, 'Hey, maybe that kid Larry Gagnon had something to do with it.' And if you did, we're going to find out. When we do, it's going to go a lot worse for you than it did today. Do you understand?"

Larry nodded. Then he felt a nudge from his mum.

"I understand, sir," he replied.

"I hope you do," the detective said. "Now you're coming with me to return the bike to its rightful owner."

They walked the bike around the side of the house. Larry watched the flashy blue paint and reflective chrome lifted into the trunk of the officer's unmarked car. Then he ducked into the passenger seat. The door closing next to him felt like a jail cell slamming shut. The detective took his time walking over to the driver's side, starting the engine, rolling slowly down the street, and rounding the familiar corners of the neighborhood. It was like riding in the belly of a shark on the prowl.

Larry still felt like that bike should belong to him. He felt that as they pulled into the driveway and Eddie and his father came out onto the porch as the detective got out. Eddie's father crossed his arms. Larry was ushered out of the car and brought around to the trunk. The detective lowered the bike into Larry's hands for the last time and told him to go give it back and apologize. Larry rolled the bike down the driveway and stopped a few feet from the porch. Eddie and his dad didn't move. They watched him carefully drop the kickstand and rest the bike before them like an offering. Larry spoke softly but directly.

"Here's your bike back. Sorry I took it."

There was a wall of silence between the father, son, and Larry. The detective nudged Larry again. "Say you're sorry louder."

"I'm sorry," Larry choked out.

Eddie came down from the porch to check out the bike for damage. He didn't even look at Larry. Neither did Eddie's father. Instead the older man sauntered up to the detective with a grin and said, "See, I told you it was the state ward, didn't I?"

The detective winced, but nodded.

Larry rode back home in the detective's car. Then he walked past his mum, Ruthie, and Clara, and into his room, shutting the door behind him. For a moment, the voice in his head stopped calling out, *Why me?* and started repeating something new over and over again, *You'll see.*

Larry never got lost in Everett. The streets guided him even before he could read the names of the roads. By the time he was old enough to notice the signs, he didn't need them. The shape of the city had grown into him, and every turn he made was second nature. Everett had a way of guiding you along wherever you were going. The great triangle of Main Street, Broadway, and Ferry Street sectioned out the neighborhoods falling on either side. The smaller tributary streets inside sloped toward one of those main thoroughfares. Even if he was in the smallest dead end of the tiniest street in the neighborhood farthest away from Swan Street Park, Larry came to know, instinctively, which direction would take him where he wanted to go. Far enough one way and you get to Route 1. Far enough the other way and you're at the Malden River. Go too far North and you hit Eastern Ave., and too far south you end up at Route 16, and then Chelsea. He grew up always knowing where he was and where he was supposed to be.

There was no better example of that than his Sundays. Larry went to church every Sunday. He knew he was Catholic, and over thousands of masses his faith grew to live deep within him. He never knew that the reason he was Catholic was because his mother had signed a piece of paper before she was deported for Canada. He didn't know that signed piece of paper may have had a part in his placement in Mrs. Giordano's house, because she was a devout Catholic as well.

All Larry knew was that there was one day a week that he got up and put on his suit, and then he walked hand in hand with his mum and Ruthie to the towering sandy red arches of the Immaculate Conception Church, which was only seven blocks away from Dean Street on Broadway. Getting into those suits was no easy task. Larry had no idea that Helen spent a great deal of her time digging up the money to pay for suits that fit, which was becoming more and more difficult as Larry started to shoot up into a beanpole with arms. It was an annual, sometimes semiannual dance between Mrs. Giordano and the social worker. She would request permission to spend money on a boy's suit. They would ask her to fit it into her existing allotment. She would explain that the allotment had been spent and that Larry had grown out of the suit already. They would ask if the suit could be adjusted for free. Mrs. Giordano would say no and they would trade phone calls until either the social worker found some money in the budget to keep Larry in church clothes, or Mrs. Giordano found another way to buy something new.

Larry and Ruthie wore a lot of hand-me-downs, but those were rarely what they put on for Sunday mass. Ruthie always had a lovely floral dress to wear for the occasion. So did Mrs. Giordano. Larry's light-colored suits complimented the group nicely. They made each church day a family portrait, walking along the sidewalks on a Sunday morning—whether or not their neighbor on Dean Street, Mr. Grant, thought to himself, "There goes Mrs. Giordano with her state wards," and whether or not they were the only family walking to the church with three different last names between them. It didn't matter. It was a special moment for all three. Mrs. Giordano made it sacred, and so did Larry and Ruthie.

Sunday Mass lasted an hour. From 9:00 a.m. to 10:00 a.m., Larry and Ruthie followed along with the service. They said the prayers, sang the hymns, and, when they were old enough, took communion. They were perfect little angels, and they did it because it pleased Mrs. Giordano and they had no choice in the matter.

Then came Sunday school. Mrs. Giordano did not go to Sunday

school, but she expected Larry and Ruthie to go. After the hour-long mass ended at 10:00 a.m., Mrs. Giordano would walk hand-in-hand with the children out into the warm glow of morning up until the fork on Broadway where they were to veer toward the church school. She would watch them go on their way together as she turned the opposite direction up toward Dean Street, where Helen would begin making a light lunch and wait for the children to return from learning their Bible.

However, there was only so much obedience in Larry and Ruthie in one day. Without Mrs. Giordano by their side, they felt the freedom of a bright morning more keenly than the desire to go into a dark classroom to study books. When their mum was safely out of sight, the two young rebels would, more often than not, do a complete 180-degree turn and march back to Broadway where the coffee shop stood waiting for Larry to pull out whatever money he'd picked up that week. He'd buy his foster sister a coffee and chocolate doughnut. They would sit together in the back corner of the shop with their brightest Sunday clothing on and enjoy their snacks until noon, when they would be expected back at the house for lunch.

If you were a regular customer at the coffee shop from 1953 to 1960, you would see the two kids there every Sunday morning. It could not be plainer to anyone that these were rogue Sunday schooler students.

By the time Larry and Ruthie turned 12, the house had changed. Clara had married an officer in the Air Force and moved overseas. As far as Ruthie was concerned, Clara may as well have been on another planet. With Larry and Ruthie getting older and more self-sufficient, Mrs. Giordano started taking in more kids. At its busiest, the Dean Street house had five foster kids: Larry, Ruthie, the twins Lee and Lenny, and the baby, Frankie. Larry took the time to be part of family time at the dinner table. After a day out, he would burst through the door with a head full of home runs and stolen bases. The other kids in the house had their stories, too. Mrs. Giordano did her best to care for each of them, but she was getting older, and it was difficult to keep up with small children. She relied on Ruthie for help, but Ruthie didn't enjoy being made into the impromptu foster mother. She had her own life to live. Larry and Ruthie did what they could to look after the other kids, but they were so much younger that Larry didn't quite know what to do.

Usually his advice was simple: "Get out of my room, go play in the yard." Benny had been an older brother to Larry. Clara had been an older sister to Ruthie. But they were both gone. Now Larry and Ruthie were the older brother and sister. They came to realize that someday they would go the way that their older brother and sister had gone—out into the wide world. The thought affected them differently at different times. Larry knew he probably wouldn't end up going to college, but figured he'd have a job somewhere. Ruthie had no idea where she would end up, but she knew she couldn't go back to her real family.

They never talked about this over coffee, though. Coffee was for comparing notes on the movies they'd caught, or joking about their adventures up at Mrs. Giordano's cabin in New Hampshire. Coffee was for sitting back and enjoying the fact that they had made their own decision about what they did with their time, and that felt good.

Helen was growing proud of Larry. His teachers at school adored him. His friends buzzed around the house. The other foster kids looked up to him. From an early age, Ruthie had a strong will and Larry was more than willing to do what Ruthie said. As the years passed, Ruthie came to see that Larry cared about her as a sister. Their inseparability became their greatest strength. Ruthie was a natural street-smart kid with a wise-guy attitude. Larry would follow her lead with all the flexibility of a freight train. No wonder the teachers separated them into different classrooms—otherwise they would have run the show.

They still walked to school together every morning and home again in the afternoon. Thanks to each other, not a single first day of school had gone by where they were so alone that they didn't know anyone in the hallways. Larry broke off to go to the park with the guys, and Ruthie came home to play with her friends. Mrs. Giordano felt that Ruthie would always be safe in the house with her and that Larry was growing up to be an upstanding young man. Little did she know Ruthie wasn't always going to be safely beneath her roof and that Larry wasn't about to stop provoking the police any time soon.

For Larry and Ruthie, the quiet moments they had to themselves in the coffee shop after Mass were their own special tradition. Larry and Ruthie didn't have the same mother and father on a birth certificate in an official government building. Whether they were fighting or not, whether grew apart or not, no matter what the future held for them, their time together had forged a simple truth: the familiar Sunday sound of a dime tapping the counter of that coffee shop after church was the sound of Larry buying a coffee for his sister. They were family.

Knowing his name was on file as a permanent person of interest at the police station changed Larry. From the time he was 12 to 13 years old, anger grew and expanded beneath the surface of everything he did, pushing even the simplest of decisions off-kilter. Instead of toeing the line to avoid the cops, he felt like he had a reputation to live up to now. His day-to-day life went from looking out for himself to looking for a way to get one over on someone else. The Swan Street Rats got bigger, too. Larry was still thin, but fiery, as he walked with the group down to the city basketball courts to play games against kids from other neighborhoods.

The gang never won those games, but they went down swinging every time. Larry and Ronnie dove after their opponents, earning a series of skinned knees and elbows from the raw impact on the asphalt. They were sandlot kids at heart basketball just wasn't as natural to them. As the games wound down and the scores looked more and more hopeless, it would inevitably become a shoving match in the paint. Then a gut punch or backhand would bring shouts and the sound of a dozen young men clattering the chain link fence around the court with fists flying.

Larry's eyes lit up in a melee. The boys around him scrambled to get out of the way, and he dove forward. His long arms swung in wide circles, connecting with the jaws of surprised bigger players. He would also bring his elbow up to a throat to pin an opponent against the fence and watch the kid's face as he tried to gut-punch his way out of it. Once the teams were dragged apart by friends, or, worse, an errant teacher who had been hanging around the courts near the school, Larry and Ronnie would move back up the hill with the guys. Sometimes it was with a cut lip or a bruise up the side of their head, but always with a sense of accomplishment on the court.

Something important had gotten out of Larry in those fights. The impact of fists had set him a little bit free, and a modicum of the anger inside him was released. He felt more freedom, but also more confused. He could feel great about ending the games like this until he came home and passed the threshold of the kitchen to see his mum's face fill with horror and anger when she saw the bruise surrounding his eye, or the blood caked on his elbow. No matter how many times he said that it was a rough game and that he was fine, he couldn't pretend he didn't know what she was thinking. She didn't want him hurt, and she didn't want him to hurt anyone else. The feeling of wanting to pound someone for pushing one of his friends and the feeling of not wanting to disappoint his mother were constantly at odds, and Larry was stuck in the middle.

That fight inside him didn't go unnoticed. He took it out onto the ball field every chance he got. When he went into the Parlin School for junior high, Coach DiBiaso told him that if he had more bulk to go with that fight, he'd be a hell of a player. Larry was a fearless athlete. Coach would put him in football games because he was fast and he didn't mind taking a few hits from the bigger guys. Even if Larry got pushed around, the other players on the team were around to bust through to the end zone. Bobby Leo was the quarterback and Richard Green played running back. Larry watched them in practice and went into each game ready to battle for every yard. He'd take the ball and run like hell. When the inevitable tackle came, followed by a pile of guys twice his size, Larry got right back up and kept at it.

Benny came to all his games. It meant something to Larry, because Benny was his idol. He'd never taken down the team photo from Boston College. It was a big deal that Benny found time to come to the games, as well. He was a busy guy. He was a teacher and he worked full afternoons and evenings for the post office. Benny and his wife Shirley had four kids, and they lived nearby, but it wasn't easy for Benny to get away. It didn't matter, though. Larry looked up to see him in the stands at every game, laughing and waving. He'd be in a group of guys who had come from the neighborhood. You could hear their outrage after each uncalled penalty from the ref, and you could see their fists raised triumphantly in the air every time Everett drove the ball ahead. Larry lived to show Benny that he belonged on that field, just like Benny had before him. There was no room for error and no time to slow down for the young athletes in Everett.

❖ ❖ ❖

Everett won. If you want a summary of the way sports went in Massachusetts, it can pretty much be summed up as, "Everett won." It's not so much a boast, or a claim, or some kind of wishful thinking. It's black-and-white history that is not up for debate. Everett High School's Crimson Tide football team was more than a school team. It was an institution that had won more state and league championships than any other team.

From 1896 to 1965, Everett won 17 state championships, including the legendary back-to-back national championship teams of 1914 and 1915. That team was so good they played 13 games in the season and never conceded a single touchdown. They outscored their opponents 600 to 0. In the 1914 national championship final, Everett beat Oak Park 80 to 0. Sure, this was a team that was almost 50 years in the past when Larry grew up, but there's a good reasons legends never die. They inspire.

The trophy case in Everett High School was in no danger of getting dusty. Everett won the state championship every year from 1961 to 1965. Larry saw them bring home three state titles by the time he was 17.

It was a big deal. It was exciting. But it was also the proper order of things as far as the kids in town were concerned. Everett was title town. And it made it that much more fun to go to games. He'd run down to the stadium with Ronnie, Bobby, Paul, and some of the guys on the team would be there. They'd see Jimmy Agnetto, Bobby Leo, and Richie Green waiting for the opening whistle with everyone else. By the time they got to high school, Bobby Leo and Richie Green had switched positions; Green was the team quarterback, and Leo was decimating defensive lines as a running back on the way to titles and a future NFL career. The two of them at a game looked like kids in a candy store. The treat they were in for was a proper thrashing of the other team, especially of their local rivals, Chelsea.

The biggest sporting event in town was the Everett vs. Chelsea game played on Thanksgiving Day. Aside from the throngs of spectators there would be at least 30 cops on duty trying to keep the peace. The trouble was, the cops wanted to see the game too, so they'd end up shouting along with the fans and if a fight were going to happen, it was just going to happen; there was nothing the police, or anyone else, could do about it. The games started for Larry with some well-timed hopping of fences while the ticket payers crowded the big main gate; then there was the line at the concession stand, and getting a good place to watch the game where you could also horse around with the guys and get in on a brawl if it broke out. Along the way, Larry got pretty good at finding places to talk to girls who had lost interest in the game too.

The outcome of the game itself was never in question; it was more a matter of how much Everett won by. Larry's class included some of the best players in the country. Bobby Leo went on to play for Harvard and then the New England Patriots. If he hadn't been on the team, the best running back would have been Lenny Canatelli, who was lightning-fast and just as strong. Needless to say, those two ran roughshod through the Chelsea defense. Richard Green was a steady hand with an eye for the perfect pass. The team was coached by Moody Sarno, who had played on the same offensive line as Vince Lombardi at Fordham University.

If a normal high school has football players who people want to take pictures of after games, Everett's football players were so good people wanted to carve them into a monument like Mount Rushmore. These were the local heroes.

At the end of Larry's junior high school career, he had a choice. He could go to the high school or he could go to the trade school. Larry didn't feel drawn by the halls of Everett High School. His teachers took him on a tour of the trade school. They showed him the machine shop and introduced him to the teachers. The building itself was a welcoming place, a short walk from home. The only downside was that the trade school didn't have a football team. In the end, Larry decided that the trade school was the place for him, and he made up for not playing football with basketball, cross-country, swimming, and hockey. And he took every chance he had to go watch the football team play. It was a big choice, but it wasn't the only important decision he made that year. The summer of 1960 turned out to be one change after another.

Helen Giordano took the family to Cape Cod for daytrips in the summer, and they spent weekends at the cabin in New Hampshire. At 15, Larry knew that most of the kids in his class spent a few weeks at camp. Some of them went to camps far away. Some of them went to ones a few miles west. Each and every one of the guys who came back had a story to tell about the fun they had. More often it was also about the girls they'd met. Beyond the kissing, there were canoeing, fishing, campfires, horsing around, and of course, playing sports.

Larry wanted in.

Like everything, summer camp cost too much. The fees for the camp were double his clothing allowance from the State, and Helen had to be direct with him about it. He was getting too old for her to guard him from the realities of his situation.

"If you want to go, you'll have to ask the social worker for more money," she said simply. "I don't have it."

Larry grimaced. The monthly visits from the social worker were not his favorite experience, and he couldn't stand talking about them, much less talking to them. The social worker would sit there with staring, judging eyes, scribbling notes. All Larry could think was, *What do you want with me anyway? Do you want to know if I'm OK? Or do you want to see if I'm not OK?* They never gave him anything except a pat on the back.

A single social worker never stayed assigned to his case long enough to get to know Larry. He could barely keep all of them straight. In fact, he was pretty sure the newest woman didn't care at all about how he was doing. She seemed to be counting down the days to when he turned 18. As she explained to him every visit, the state's interest was that Larry get a job and leave the house. That explanation became more emphatic when Larry entered the trade school and started studying sheet metal fabrication.

"Now that you're learning a vocation, the next step is to plan where you want to work when you leave," the social worker said. Larry couldn't even remember her name.

"Leave where?" Larry asked.

"Leave the state's care," she explained. "At 18, the law is that you age out of the system. The government support for Mrs. Giordano to care for you stops."

"You mean you'll kick me out," Larry said.

"Not exactly …" Her eyes searched the wall and Larry thought, *That's exactly what she means.* Larry searched the social worker's face for some other interpretation of what "aging out of the system" meant. There wasn't any.

Helen appeared in the living room doorway. She had been listening and was clearly ready to say something. Larry's mum had an anger in her demeanor that he recognized. He was glad to see it directed at the social worker this time. Helen sent a cold stare toward the visitor in the corner and then turned to fix her eyes on Larry.

"You have a place to stay here for as long as you like, Larry, whether I get support or not. This is your house too," she said, adding, "and I've told the workers that many times before." She gave the social worker another intimidating look and returned to the kitchen.

The social worker cleared her throat and returned her attention to Larry, with a much softer tone.

"That's very kind of Helen, I mean Mrs. Giordano," she stumbled. "Legally, you will be aged out of the system at 18, though, and it would be best if you had a job to support yourself." The message was loud and clear—18 and out.

So Larry threw himself into his work at the trade school and his side jobs delivering groceries for Montello's Market, delivering heating oil with Louis Rosenthal, and the two paper routes. Once Ronnie started driving, they could deliver more papers with Larry leaning out of the window of the moving car and chucking papers onto porches as they passed. He really started to get some cash together. A lot of it went to hockey equipment and to fares for the blue bus down to Revere Beach or the pool. More was divided up with the guys for whatever they needed at the time. He was determined to show the social worker and his mum that if he was allowed to stay at the house, then he was going to be independent. He worked so hard at all these jobs that the social worker found out about it from Larry's teachers at the trade school. Before long, Helen got a phone call asking for Larry to come into the social worker's office in Boston the next day.

That had never happened before. Helen tried to shrug off a sense of uncertainty. Now that she had four foster kids in the house, the usual way of things had been to let Larry be while she fussed about the little ones. Larry didn't need to be watched constantly anymore, and he could more than hold his own with a social worker in their office in Boston. Still, she could guess he was probably in for another lecture about leaving home. She decided that she would arm him with the confidence that he wasn't leaving her house.

After dinner, she called Larry into the living room where he usually interviewed with the social worker. Larry lounged on the couch, his torn jeans and beat-up canvas shoes stretched from the cushions to the carpet as his arms dangled comfortably at his sides. Helen sat up straight and crossed her ankles beneath her seat. She took off her glasses and looked directly into Larry's eyes. Her gaze was something familiar, but greater in a way than Larry had seen before. He could sense the importance of her voice and the emotion poured outward from her heart.

"The social worker called today," she said. "They'd like you to come into Boston for a meeting."

Larry's eyes narrowed suspiciously. Helen nodded her head, as if agreeing that it was important to be suspicious around the state office. That wasn't the most important thing, though. She had something she needed him to understand as he got older.

"Listen to me, Larry," She said. "Your last name is Gagnon. My last name is Giordano. That is the only difference between us and any other family. I don't care what this state says. I don't care what the law is. This is your house. We are your family and …"

Helen's lip gave a hint of a quiver but she caught herself up to continue.

"I am your mother."

Larry lifted himself from his slouching position. He leaned forward with his arms crossed and resting on his knees. His heart was filled to bursting and he nodded his agreement. Helen stood up. So did Larry. The two never hugged, but a solemnity passed between them and wrapped around Larry's shoulders like a blanket.

He wore that conversation like a shield as he took the trip into the social worker's office. His mum was right. This was all paperwork. The real law was written on Dean Street, and the proof was in the years and years of her caring for him every day. He knew that wasn't going to end when he turned 18. But, then again, neither of them knew what was waiting for Larry in that office.

Larry went into Boston reassured, but nervous nonetheless. He'd seen enough of his fellow foster kids packed up and moved with little to no warning. There was no reason to believe that couldn't happen to him. "She's my mum," he said to himself over and over again, praying that there was nothing this social worker could write down that would change that. "She's my mum and it's my house."

Taking the trolley made Larry feel a mixture of happiness and loneliness. He remembered being younger and throwing heavy sticks at the electrical arms above the moving cars. If he could hit them hard enough, it brought the trolley to a dead stop. He would laugh with the guys as the driver cussed them out and used his radio to call for help. It took a while for the guys to hook the trolley arm back into place to get it running again. Larry and the guys would watch from a distance and laugh. The memories of that laughter were followed closely by the fear that he felt over what the state had in store for him.

He was happy to be Larry Gagnon and have a mum like Helen Giordano. Despite all of the intrepid attitude and the confidence that he tried to show to the guys at the park, the teachers at school, and the other kids at the house, he knew he was alone when it came to this. In that office up the long stairwell in a brick building, the state was his only parent. The state was the strange force that paid for his doctor visits and Sunday suits. Now he was being called to the seat of its power for a meeting and he had no idea what to expect behind the heavy wooden doors.

He certainly didn't expect what he found. The social worker who had sat in his mum's living room and explained to him about getting a job to leave home was waiting in a small office that appeared to be shared with someone else. Papers were stacked up behind her, and Larry wondered if they were all the notes that had been written about him over the years. Somehow he felt, looking at the social worker suspiciously, that those documents were part of a countdown to when Larry would be off of their books. He wondered if the office would erupt into applause on Larry's 18th birthday and all those folders would be thrown from the window in a ticker tape parade as Larry was forced out of his mum's house.

"Come in and sit down, Larry," the social worker said. Larry didn't want to, but he did. And when he lowered himself into the chair he saw there, on the desk, was a framed photo. It was yellowed at the edges, and showed a nurse in a clean white uniform. She wore a flat cap and she and held a baby wrapped in a white blanket, his tiny body bundled up helplessly. A concerned brow accented his round face and wide eyes. The baby stared out of the photo and into the social worker's office at Larry, who tried not to let on that he was curious. He didn't want to give anything of himself up to the social worker, but there was something about the baby that made Larry think that the social worker knew more about him than he knew about himself.

"That's you, Larry," he said. "At three weeks old."

She leaned in closer, elbows on the desk, watching Larry react. She smiled a smile that resembled caring, but it presented itself more like a fascination. Larry glanced at the photo again. The youngest pictures he'd seen of himself had been at his mum's house. There was a picture of him at 3 years old playing on a swing. This photo was new, though. This was Larry before he lived on Dean Street. He looked at the nurse holding the baby and he wondered if it could actually be true.

"You know it says in your file that you have never asked about your real parents," the social worker said. Larry forced himself to look away from the photo to the nameplate on the other side of the desk: J.E. Gould. So he was talking to Mrs. Gould. It helped him to look at the social worker and see a name instead of a stranger who had stockpiled Larry's baby pictures.

"Have you ever been curious about your real parents?" Mrs. Gould asked.

Larry looked away and shook his head, partly because even though he had been curious about his parents, he didn't want to give this woman the satisfaction of saying so, and partly because, even though he thought about his parents all the time, it was more important to him that he stayed on Dean Street with his mum. He didn't even understand the concept of having real parents. He had always been at Helen's house. That was it. She was as real a mum as he had ever had or could ever need.

But Mrs. Gould wasn't satisfied: "You know, it's important that you don't hide your feelings about these things. If you want to know about your real parents, all you have to do is ask. If you don't, it could bother you your whole life."

Larry didn't reply. He didn't think very much about his whole life. At the moment he was focused on his life right now, his life in this office and how soon he could be out of it and get into a summer camp. He returned his gaze to the photo. He let himself believe in a strange world where that confused little baby was him, and this nurse was holding him while someone pointed a camera at them. He peered closer at the baby, at its expression, its little nose.

"This was taken in Springfield, Mass.," Mrs. Gould said.

"I've never been to Springfield," Larry shot back without thinking.

"Yes, you have. You went there right after you were born. That's where your real mother left you in a hotel room."

Larry felt like his heart stopped in his chest. Mrs. Gould continued.

"Your real mother wasn't in a position to raise you, Larry. So she left you in a hotel. Her family didn't approve of her having a baby so she left you here before she was sent back to Canada. You became a ward of the state."

"State ward," Larry whispered, curling the side of his lip into a mocking grin. "And then I went to my mum's house."

"Not at first. You spent three years with another foster parent; she was more of an infant caretaker. That was an apartment in Roxbury. You aged into Mrs. Giordano's house after that."

Larry looked at the photo again. "I lived in Roxbury," he breathed. "I've been to Springfield." He didn't remember it, of course, and he didn't actually believe it. This was all an interesting story to him now, like a science fiction movie. The social worker shuffled through a couple more papers.

"Do you ever wonder about your father?" Mrs. Gould asked. It was always a concern for cases like this. Young men without father figures were difficult. She had asked the question to see Larry's response. Her answer was carefully prepared if Larry wanted to know.

"Yes," Larry said.

"He was a mechanic in the Army. He and your mother met at a base in Maine. He shipped out to Europe before you were born." She paused and watched Larry for signs of interest. Then she continued. "Are you looking forward to learning a trade at school?"

"Yes," Larry said, but he wasn't thinking about school right now. He was wondering what happened to his father in the war.

"Well, I suppose that runs in the family then, Larry. Your father was a mechanic, and from what I understand, he was a good one. He served our country in uniform. Is that something you might like to do?"

Larry looked up. "You mean be a mechanic or join the army?"

"Both," answered Mrs. Gould. "You could do both if you enter the service."

Larry didn't answer. He leaned back. As far as he knew, his two real parents were still alive out there in the world somewhere. He wanted to ask, but the look on Mrs. Gould's face said their conversation was about to change again.

"Larry, listen. I know you've started working some jobs," she said. "It's important for all of that money to be recorded in your file."

Larry tilted his head. "What jobs?" he asked.

"Let me see, we know you've been delivering groceries and I also heard you have a paper route," she flipped through a pad to confirm that those things were written in her notes. "Is that right?"

Larry stared at the ceiling for a while without answering. He was glad Louis Rosenthal's oil truck wasn't on her note pad. At least he still had a few secrets. Mrs. Gould cleared her throat and Larry piped up.

"What do you mean they have to be recorded?" he asked.

"I mean that the money you are making now needs to be in your record so we know you can hold down a job," she replied. "So we know you're saving. It's a good thing."

There was a long pause during which Larry felt highly skeptical that it was a good thing at all. Larry had learned that it was rarely a good thing to tell anyone, except your friends, how much money you had. Mrs. Gould could tell he was clamming up so she shook her head and explained further.

"It also means that, thanks to your hard work, Mrs. Giordano might not have to accept as much government support."

And there it is, Larry thought. *They're always working an angle.*

"I'll get you a tally or something," Larry said, slowly. "Mum makes me save it all so there's money in the bank already. But it's just the paper route, Mr. Aiosa doesn't use kids for groceries anymore." Larry thought it would be best not to let on he had a job that frequently paid him in cases of beer that he would share with the guys in the park. He thought about those kinds of paydays and looked placidly at Mrs. Gould and said, "I don't get money for that."

"You do get money for the paper route, though," Mrs. Gould insisted.

"Yeah, I do," Larry said, tapping his fingers on the edge of the desk. He let the room go silent for a moment. "But I have something else on my mind."

"What's that?" asked Mrs. Gould.

"I'd like to go to camp, like the other kids," Larry said.

Mrs. Gould leaned back and let out a puff of air. She had started this conversation to find out what kind of resources her department could redirect from this kid and here he was trying to get more money from her. "Okay, which camp?"

"There's one run by the Monsignor at our church. It's called Cedar something. It's on the South Shore."

"Why is that interesting for you?" the social worker asked.

Larry shrugged his shoulders. "All the other guys get to go. I've never been."

"Well, how much is it?"

Larry shrugged again. "It's more than I can afford on a paper route."

Mrs. Gould chuckled. She shut her eyes for a moment and leaned back in her chair.

"Okay," she sighed, "I'll see what I can do."

Larry nodded.

"Can I go now?" he asked, getting up and heading for the door.

"Sure, sure, but get me that number of how much is in the bank and how much you make a month will you," she said. "And another thing Larry …"

The young man turned back with his hand on the open door.

"Don't forget to think about your future."

"Yeah," Larry said, and walked out into the hallway, visions of camp clouded out by a nurse's uniform and the questioning look of a baby in Springfield.

Camp Cedarcrest was the life's work of Monsignor Hartigan, a tall, stern, silver-haired priest who had a vision for giving the children in his parish a beautiful outdoor space to enjoy while they learned about scripture and cemented their position in the church over years of attendance before graduating and moving on to work or college. It was actually two camps, separated by a hill with cedar trees at the top. Boys were on one side and girls were on the other. The planning that went into sneaking back and forth was the life's work of many campers. Fortunately boys and girls all ate together at one dining hall and there were camp dances that got everyone together. Otherwise, it was separate recreation halls, separate buses to the beach, and, most definitely, separate bunks.

It was only an hour south on route 3. Larry's first sight of the white lettering on the sign spelling out Camp Cedarcrest accompanied the slamming of the camp counselor's car door as he got out of the van on a steaming hot day. Aside from the small stand of trees on the hill there wasn't much shade around. It was mostly open farm fields. The cabins in the distance were spread out like teepees in a Western. A college kid camp counselor walked Larry up to the camp office, which was separated from the parking area by a short staircase. The office cabin was a modest single-floor building with a few windows on either side of the doorway leading to a few desks where the camp directors waited for parents dropping off campers.

Larry approached the reception desk. "Hello," he said. The woman behind the desk looked up at the thin boy standing before her and put on her spectacles.

"Name please?" she asked.

"Larry Gagnon."

The secretary perked up. "Gagnon?" She feigned confusion before putting her hands on a separate slip of paper and reading it over carefully. "You're the charity boy, aren't you?"

Larry again at the old floorboards and then looked up. "Yes, ma'am," he said, without changing the calm expression on his face. Inside, he was burnt to be called a charity case.

"Did they explain the rules that your social worker and Monsignor Hartigan worked out?" she asked.

"Yes, ma'am," Larry nodded.

The secretary wasn't convinced though, or perhaps, she wanted to go over them again with him. Larry watched her take off her glasses as she looked him over.

"You are to do extra cleanup work in the dining hall and in the kitchen after meals before you return to camp activities," she explained.

Larry's eyes betrayed a hint of alarm. "I thought I was to clean up for one hour after the dinner."

The secretary tapped her pencil to the card. "That's not what I have here, so we will check with the Monsignor to clarify. In any event, you are here to help out with the staff before going out to the camp. That means you can attend the camp at no cost to your foster mother ..."

Larry nodded, but the secretary wasn't done.

"... or to the state."

Larry felt as if there may as well have been a brand on his forehead that said, "State Ward." He didn't feel welcome, but he still wanted to be there. He could see the cabins in the distance; he was so close to going like the other kids. He could hear the shouts of them playing. He hoped it would be worth it.

"Are we all clear on the rules?" the secretary asked.

"Yes, ma'am," Larry nodded.

"Good," she chirped. "One of the counselors will be here shortly to show you to your cabin."

In no time, Larry was carrying his shopping bag full of clothes and his toothbrush across an open lawn and through stands of trees toward the lake. The camp counselors were all kids who had been at Cedarcrest every summer since they were 8 years old. Even the regular campers Larry's age were mostly return customers who had already gotten to know the paths and knew all the best games in the recreation hall. Their bunks had been claimed already. They were hanging out with their friends. They were like a neighborhood gang that didn't take kindly to someone new arriving. Larry knew the feeling well.

Larry's tall, lanky frame; mussed sneakers; and old shopping bag full of clothes didn't match all the other campers who wore comfortable summer clothes and stacked duffel bags on their bunks. More than a few fingers pointed at that shopping bag. The counselors whispered to one another that this was the State Ward. Again, Larry could sense it all around him. But he was more excited to finally be there to see what really went on. The cabins didn't have doors on them so the counselors could keep track of everyone, and each bunk had a shelf beside for the kids to keep their things. Larry dropped his bag and set off exploring.

He walked up the hill, surveying the open fields dotted with cows in the distance. Halfway up, he came across a clean white statue of Mary with praying sculptures around her. Later, he'd discover that the shrine to Mary was one of the places the seminarians held classes during the camp. Without knowing that, he felt like he'd discovered an open-air church, with the sky as the cathedral ceiling. Larry walked among the kids as they went from program to program, recognizing some of them from the few Sunday school classes he hadn't skipped out on. He recognized others from hockey at the Elm Street Rec Center or swimming at the pool. They would nod at each other in recognition, but Larry was still the new kid, even in a camp filled with people from Everett.

Morning programs were seminary lessons. Larry paid attention to them as well as he did in school. Fortunately, there was no homework. Then they'd hit the recreation hall to check out some sports equipment. There weren't enough gloves for multiple games to be going on out in the fields. Larry had brought his, but at first he wasn't eager to take it out because it was so old and beat up. After a few hours playing, it was time for lunch.

The midday meal started with an unholy ruckus as kids piled into the dining hall. It was the first time the boys and girls had been together since Larry arrived, and Larry got along with the girls better than the guys. Some of them had been friends of his at the Lincoln School. There wasn't much time to talk because lunch only lasted as long as it took for a couple hundred kids to shove food in their faces and run out the door. The counselors were rushing them back outside so the staff could clean up and get ready for dinner.

By the time the afternoon classes and programs were over, the dining hall had to be restocked with trays of spaghetti or lasagna. Those were the raw materials of another brutal mess that would be created when the kids descended back into the dining hall. After dinner, the campers split up again, and the girls went back to their side of the hill. The boys would go out to sing songs around a campfire before going to bed.

The counselors would try to get people to talk about what they did that day as a group, but it mostly devolved into chaotic chatter. Every kid talked to every other kid until the lights went out and they got a bit of sleep to do it all over again. Once a week, the campers piled into a truck and went for a daytrip to the beach. That was the highlight of each week, especially in the heat.

Despite the gender separation, campers were coupling up. Rumors about who was dating whom were top-level gossip. Dating was the main focus of camp for most of the kids there. But Larry soon came to learn that his experience was not going to be like everyone else's. On the dirt path between the recreation hall and the dining hall, one of the boys caught up with him and asked, "Hey, are you the charity case?"

"I'm not getting in for free. They're making me work in the kitchen," Larry said.

"Yeah I know, everyone washes dishes, but the charity cases wash the pots and pans in the kitchen too," the boy replied.

"I'm just doing what they told me," Larry said.

"So why are you a charity case? Is your family poor or something?"

"No," Larry started. The boy seemed to lose interest and skipped off to some other guys. He started talking to them about what he'd found out. Larry sat with the same guys at lunch and dinner the first day. On the second day, he felt a hand grasp his shoulder. "You're Larry Gagnon?" a gruff voice asked.

Larry turned to see the head of the kitchen staff towering over him.

"Yes, sir," he said.

"Fine, well after you're done and you've scrubbed your dishes, you come over to that door and we'll put you to work in the kitchen, okay?"

As he said it, Larry felt the hall go quiet, there was a short calm before the voices picked up again, spiking in volume as Larry stood and shuffled over to the kitchen door as he had been instructed. He didn't know why. He'd been making money one way or another since he was 7, but there was something about the eyes watching him go to work, something that made camp feel the opposite of someplace in nature that was big and open. It felt like a trap.

The kitchen workers were nice to Larry. They would joke around about the hard life and say things like, "Welcome to Camp Scrubbing Pans." Larry was up to his elbows in dirty dishwater with more filthy trays waiting on the counters around him than he could count. There wasn't a clock in the room, but Larry knew he wasn't supposed to be doing this for more than an hour. The sounds of kids in the dining hall came and went. Soon, the rest of the campers were long gone and he could hear them outside. Their yells echoed along on the path back to the cabins and from the recreation hall. Still, there were endless trays to clean. The final bin to land in his sink was filled with plates and utensils.

"I thought everyone cleaned their own?" Larry said.

"Those are the staff dishes, last batch for the lunch hour."

Larry saw that everyone else who had been in the kitchen was done and gone. Some of the kids who had gotten too old to attend as students had come back as waiters in the dining hall. They were gone. It was just Larry and the cooks. Larry cleaned; the cooks were working on dinner already. If it weren't for all the disgusting food Larry had just scrubbed off pots and pans, he would have been hungry again after all that work. Larry started to wash the plates and silverware, but the head of the kitchen staff, who was named Tom, stopped him.

"C'mon kid, you can't use the dirty pan water for those. Drain it and fill it with clean water and soap for the plates and forks."

So Larry pulled the stopper out of the sink, drained the water, and watched what must have been the slowest sink on earth fill up with for the next, and hopefully final, round. The time in the kitchen had dragged on so long that the angles of sunlight outline reminded him of how the sky looked when it was time for dinner on Dean Street. Finally the dishes were done and stacked. The head of the kitchen staff clapped Larry on the back and handed him a broom. "Now sweep up the hall on your way out for me, kid. Then we're all set."

Larry's face dropped. "The whole dining hall?" he lamented.

"It won't sweep itself, kid. Don't worry, you'll get fast at all this soon. No problem."

Larry watched as the rest of the kitchen staff took their aprons off and went outside for a breath of fresh air, something he had no time for. Instead it was he and the broom and a dining hall strewn with debris after the vicious lunch rush. By the time he finished sweeping up all the crumbs, most of the kids were back in the cabins getting ready to go to dinner. A couple of guys were throwing a football around on the lawn beside the recreation hall. A group of girls were seated up on the hill getting a lesson from a seminarian. The sleeves of Larry's rolled-up shirt were wet. His hands were pruned from the dishwater.

"How was that for you, huh?" asked the same kid who had come to find out about Larry the day before.

"They kept me longer than I thought today," Larry said.

"No joking about that mess, huh," the kid laughed. Larry couldn't feel anything but anger.

"Hey, better you than me," the guy grinned. Suddenly the

familiar sound of the voice of the Boston Red Sox, Curt Gowdy, reached their ears. The boy turned with a shout.

"Donnie's got his radio out!"

Larry followed him over to the shade beside a cabin where a circle of boys sat around Donnie, who was moving the antenna of a compact radio about the size of a pencil box. It was made of clean blue plastic. The sounds of the game pierced the humid summer air. Suddenly, those wild cheers of Fenway fans were transported to Camp Cedarcrest. Larry stood and listened to the game with them for a while. The crack of the bat was crystal clear as Don Buddin struck a double against the Kansas City Athletics. It was the second of a four-game series in Boston, and the night before the Athletics had scored 10 runs against the Sox. Larry leaned in, hoping to hear Ted Williams was up next, and he was about to say so when Donnie put a finger to his lips and shook his head.

"Quiet down, kid," he hissed, even though Larry hadn't even had a chance to speak.

Larry listened with the rest of them to the double play that ended the inning. The game went on to end with 10 more runs against the Sox and the second loss in a row, but Larry didn't stick around to hear the last inning. He ran back to the cabin to get his mitt, figuring if he could get those guys into a game then he'd show them a thing or two. By the time he got back out, the bats and balls had been locked up for the day. There were only a few minutes left until the campers were called back to the dining hall for supper.

It was like a recurring bad dream. Larry trudged back to the same table and sat on his baseball glove to pick at some dry spaghetti. He waited in fear for Tom from the kitchen staff to come get him. Almost immediately after the kids had been served, here came the big guy to drag Larry back to the dishwashing basin. There, once again, a mountain of trays piled up around him while the din of children at their tables faded away and the sun dipped over the hill behind the cedar trees. Tom didn't leave him alone while he washed, either.

"Hey kid, those floors didn't look so good after lunch. Don't miss so many spots this time," he said, nodding to the dining area. Once again, Larry worked his way around the tables with the broom, making sure to get everywhere and then put the chairs back in place for another day of meals and cleaning. Then Larry walked back to his cabin where he shuffled into the dimly lit bunks with his baseball mitt in tow.

"Late game, slugger?" Donnie asked from the other side of the cabin. The boy stifled his own laughter while the guys around him cracked up. Larry waved him off and threw his mitt onto the shelf by his bunk. At this rate, he was better off at the park. He hadn't played a single minute and the closest he'd gotten to talking to a girl was a few words at lunch before being dragged off to kitchen duty. He went to the bathrooms, brushed his teeth, came back to bed and stared at the ceiling, missing Swan Street Park. When he finally drifted off, he fell into fitful dreams of dried marinara sauce on beat-up metal trays. The boos of the Fenway faithful bounced around the dining hall as Larry swept up after dozens of ungrateful campers.

By the third day at camp, Larry was fed up. The dishes and the sweeping had been awful. The guys froze him out of the games because he was always late getting out of the kitchen. Nothing was going his way … well, *most* things weren't going his way. There were a couple of girls who would wait for him to get out of the kitchen and catch him up on what he had missed: a redhead named Joanne and a cute brunette named Marguerite. Larry would tease them about hanging out with him. "I'm just a damn dishwasher," he would say, but they didn't seem to mind.

Larry tried to make the best of things. Despite all the work in the kitchen, he did get to spend time in the recreation hall. He could also get some games together outside with the younger kids in the morning. Before long, he had a pretty good group going. They liked having one of the older kids leading the game, and it wasn't too far off from what Larry was used to at the park. Every home run was in the park since they played on a gigantic, empty field. Larry liked seeing the ball arch into the distance and bounce in the turf. It was a change of pace from always having to send kids to climb fences after a home run.

The kid who had found out Larry was the "charity case" was named Frankie, short for Francis. The guy with the radio was Donnie. Frankie and Donnie never missed an opportunity to ask how the dishwashing was going. When they saw Larry leading a game with the younger campers, they called him the baby counselor.

"You get kicked out of your home there, counselor? Washing dishes and coaching ball for a living?" Frankie would ask.

"Why don't you coach those kids into washing some dishes for you, sport?" called out Donnie.

Larry let their voices trail off. A couple of times he came close to decking Frankie, but the whole camp seemed like church to him. He'd never get into a fight at church, so he wasn't about to get into one here. He wasn't planning on throwing in the towel, either. Calling Mum to go home seemed like a good idea sometimes, but he hadn't spent enough time with the girls yet. He hadn't even gone to the beach. There was too much pride in him to quit, or maybe too much fight. He took a careful mental picture of each guy who gave him grief, remembering the pattern of freckles on Frankie's cheeks and the combed pattern of Donnie's hair. Everett was a small town, and Larry knew he'd cross paths with them again, hopefully on the basketball court with the rest of the Swan Street Rats. He'd get even.

The idea kept him going through all the dishwashing and sweeping, and Tom added another job—dragging the trash out to the big dumpster. That earned Larry a new nickname from his peanut gallery: "garbage man." They would shout it from the windows of the recreation center after every meal while Larry was working. Without trees or houses to block the sound, the call of "gaaarbage maaaaan" drifted all the way to the kitchen, where Larry cursed under his breath, kicked a few of the trays stacked beside him, and kept working.

Joanne thought the other boys were horrible. She would tell them to shush or let Larry know not to mind the big jerks because they didn't matter anyway. At the same time, she was curious, and even though Larry hated talking about not having parents, she seemed like someone he could trust. Or maybe he just wanted someone to talk to. They'd go for walks up the hill to Mary's shrine. Larry kicked clumps of dirt along the way while Joanne asked questions.

"Is it true you don't have parents?"

Larry looked at her sharply. "I got my mum," he said.

"But she's not your real mother," Joanne ventured, tilting her head to see how Larry reacted.

"Well, she's real enough for me."

"What happened to your real mother?"

"Hell if I know," Larry kicked another clump of dirt and watched it explode on the end of his sneaker. "I was a baby. Who says I don't have parents anyway? Who told you that?"

"Everyone knows you're the state ward, Larry."

"Who said that?"

"Donnie was telling Marguerite."

Larry snorted: "Well, Donnie's an asshole, alright." He left her there on the side of the hill and walked back to the recreation hall. Joanne thought about chasing after him, but she knew there would be more chances to talk to him. She hadn't meant to upset him. She was only curious about the boy with no mother.

Back down at the bottom of the hill, Larry bumped into one of the younger kids, a nice one named George. "You seen that kid Donnie, George?" Larry asked.

"Sure, he was heading to the shower," the younger boy pointed to the shower cabin. "You want me to tell him you're looking for him next time I run into him?"

"Nah," Larry said, and turned toward the sleeping cabin where he knew Donnie must have left his radio. *He wouldn't take it with him to the shower*, Larry thought, *but I'd better be quick*.

The showers at Camp Cedarcrest must have been fed directly from Antarctica. The water was frigid. Even though they were supposed to shower every day, the younger kids would often splash their faces and hair, and then stick their towels in the water to make it look like they'd showered so the counselors wouldn't make them go back for more. Chances were, Donnie wouldn't be gone long at all.

Larry waited for the counselor by the cabin to turn his back before slipping through the side door and running over to Donnie's bunk. The blue radio was under Donnie's duffel bag, barely concealed. In no time, Larry had it in his baseball mitt and trotted out to the recreation hall with the mitt under his arm. Behind him, a counselor waved hello, none the wiser.

Larry's stride quickened and there was a bounce in his step as he found a secluded spot beside the storage shed and carefully turned on the radio, keeping it set to the lowest volume. Larry held it up to his ears and heard the faintest sound of the Red Sox thrashing the Washington Senators. He sat with his back against the wooden siding, listening to the game and basking in the open space around him. A beautiful red sun dipped into distant low clouds, warming the deep blue sky. Larry knew what he had just done, and he knew there was a chance this was his last sunset at camp. He'd spent more time in the kitchen or alone in the bunks than he had at the beach swimming, but this was worth it to him.

Donnie was going to come back from the shower and find that the radio was gone. The "garbage man" had gotten even. Before Larry knew it, the dinner bell rang. He shut off the radio and hid the shiny blue casing in his baseball glove before trotting off to dinner like it was any other night. And, just like every other night, Larry had barely finished his food when Tom brought him back into the kitchen to start in on the dishes.

Larry carefully placed his baseball mitt on the windowsill in the corner of the kitchen as he got to work. Outside, the sounds of campers in a feeding frenzy died away as everyone left and Larry went about his normal routine with one eye on his baseball glove on the corner. He worked through all the pots and pans. The trays were washed and stacked neatly in their place. Tom had just brought the staff dishes to Larry's sink when a counselor ran into the kitchen, slamming the door behind him and rolling his eyes.

"What's going on?" asked Tom.

"Some kid is having a meltdown because his transistor radio is missing. Everyone's losing their minds looking for it."

Larry kept his head down and his hands in the dishes. He strained to contain a vindicated smile. Not only was the radio safely out of reach from anyone in the bunks, Larry was nowhere near the commotion. He finished the dishes and started sweeping, thinking about where he could hide the radio on the way back to the bunk. He thought about putting it in the supply closet or slipping it under the dishwashing sink. Maybe he could climb a cedar tree at the top of the hill and leave it up there. He preferred to keep it close, though. After all, what was the point of having it if he wasn't able to listen to the games? He figured that he would try to find somewhere outside the cabin on the way back to the bunk. When the sweeping was done, Larry propped the broom back up against the wall and walked over to the windowsill. He put his hand out to grab the baseball mitt.

Just then, the kitchen door swung open to reveal the looming figure of Monsignor Hartigan. Larry had seen him every morning during seminary lessons, but this was the first time he'd seen the priest up close. The Monsignor wore crisp, straight slacks and his priest collar on a dark shirt with the sleeves rolled up past the elbow to keep him cool in the warm summer night. The dark wilderness outside clashed with the man's silver hair and thin, metal-rimmed spectacles. The Monsignor fixed his attention on Larry and strode over in his direction. In spite of himself, Larry stepped back in surprise. More figures appeared in the doorway. Donnie rushed in behind the priest with Frankie and some of the other boys in tow.

"That's him, he's got it!" Donnie accused, pointing to Larry, who froze. Larry hoped the radio's blue plastic wasn't visible through the leather seams of his glove.

"I'll handle this young man," Monsignor Hartigan said, holding his palm out to silence Donnie, who was exasperated. The priest was calm and quiet, allowing a long pause to settle in the kitchen while Joe and the staff looked on with interest. Finally, the Monsignor strode over to Larry, looking at him carefully. Larry knew he would have to be perfect to bluff his way out of this one.

"It's Larry, isn't it?" Monsignor Hartigan asked.

Larry nodded. He waited as the square-jawed man prepared to speak again.

"This young man's blue transistor radio has gone missing and he's hoping to find it. Do you know anything about it?" Behind the priest, Donnie shot daggers at Larry.

"No, sir," Larry said.

"To be clear, he's convinced you've taken it."

Larry's features betrayed nothing. He looked at the ceiling past the priest to keep from giving any indication that he knew where the radio had gone. Monsignor Hartigan continued.

"Do you have the radio, Larry?"

"No, sir," Larry said. "You can search my stuff."

The priest's eyes narrowed and he put his hand to his chin in a bemused way. There was another long pause. Donnie couldn't keep quiet this time: "Where did you put it, pal?! I know you have it somewhere!"

Again, the priest put out a hand to calm the other boy. "We already looked for it with your belongings in the bunk and it was not there. So it is very possible you do not have it after all," he said.

Larry nodded his agreement. It certainly was possible that he didn't have it. And that meant that he should probably be able to go. He didn't move though. He hadn't been dismissed and he didn't know whether he should nonchalantly pick up his baseball glove or to leave it there and hope nobody noticed it. There was a flash of recognition in the priest and he took off his spectacles before speaking again.

"Is that your baseball glove?" he asked, indicating to the one behind Larry on the windowsill.

The game was up.

Larry nodded.

"May I ask why you brought it to your kitchen duty today?"

Larry shrugged.

"I would like to take a look at it, please."

Larry stepped aside as the priest lifted the glove and opened it to see its contents. He was not relieved finding the radio there. He seemed more aggrieved than he would have been if the radio had never been recovered.

"I see," he said, passing the radio to Donnie, who exhaled a breath of relief before spitting on the floor and storming out with Frankie and the others. Larry barely watched them go. His eyes stayed down. Monsignor Hartigan paced to the window to watch the crowd of boys chattering as they returned to the bunks. He motioned for the kitchen staff to leave before turning his attention back to Larry.

"You were allowed to attend camp under certain conditions. It seems as though you have not upheld your part of the bargain, Larry." Larry continued to look away.

The priest paced some more and then went on. "I think they were entirely reasonable conditions to meet, but nonetheless, you are not suitable to stay in camp now."

"You've got to be kidding me," Larry blurted out.

"Excuse me?"

"This isn't even a camp, it's a dump."

"Are you criticizing our generosity?" the priest bristled.

"I've done enough dishes this week to last a lifetime. Way more than an hour a day. I want to go home."

The Monsignor's eyes widened for a moment and then he seemed to remember himself, and perhaps more about Larry. He walked to the door. "We will be calling your foster mother to inform her of the circumstances under which you are leaving. You will be driven home first thing in the morning."

Larry felt a wave of regret. He pictured the disappointment in his mum's face seeing him back at the camp office. He was contrite, truly, in that moment. "Please don't tell her about the radio," he begged. All the old fears of being taken away from the house on Dean Street came back. The fear returned and poured forth from Larry as he pleaded. "Don't tell her about this. Tell her I just want to leave, that I don't like it here."

Monsignor Hartigan had thought about a great deal while watching Larry. He had thought about his conversation with the social worker. He had thought about his commitment to lift up all the members of the church. He had thought about his dedication to the camp and the unrest this one boy had brought to Cedarcrest by stealing the radio. He thought about the future of this young man, and wondered how he would hear of him or see him next. There seemed a good chance it would not be for something positive. In his time, living through the Great War, he had seen young men of all kinds go through difficulties. This young man's journey had been difficult, and it was just beginning.

Monsignor Hartigan thought about all of these things, but he did not think for a moment about telling Mrs. Giordano anything but the truth. He shook his head and called for the camp counselor who was to be in charge of settling Larry into a cot in the staff cabin. He wasn't even allowed to return to the boys' bunks. His shopping bag full of clothing was brought to him. Larry lay awake all night listening to the snores of the counselors. When the sun finally rose, he took his things and walked his way to the camp office where one of the counselors waited lazily by the camp's white van. Larry walked out to the curb and got in.

After a short drive home from a short trip to camp, Larry was back on Dean Street. He dragged his bag into the entryway and collapsed on the couch despairingly. His mum had been told. On cue, she turned the corner from the kitchen doorway and observed Larry with a severe look.

"I'm sorry, mum," Larry sighed.

Her severity softened. She turned away from him and returned to the kitchen. "Put your things away and come have breakfast."

Larry sat up and looked over to the empty kitchen doorway in amazement. He had expected to receive the full treatment, complete with the green broom. He stood up tentatively and picked up his things. As he made his way up to his room, his mum emerged from the kitchen again and looked up at him on the stairway.

"It's good to have you back at the house, Larry," she said softly. Larry nodded. The best part about camp was definitely coming home.

Larry started at the trade school in the fall. It was a comfortable series of classrooms where he got a chance to get to work on engines and building projects along with the long classes in which he sat at the back of the room and chatted with a few of the pretty girls who were kind enough help him manage his homework.

One of his favorite teachers was Mr. O'Neil, who taught math. The first lesson of the day was picking winners from the racing forms. They'd find out how their picks had done in the papers the next day. Larry got used to a more relaxed kind of class.

The sports, on the other hand, were a different story. Larry might not have been the biggest guy at the high school, but he was in demand at the trade school. He joined the basketball team, where he got a taste of what it was like to play with a referee breathing down his neck. He cut the fists and elbows out of his game and focused on moving fast and keeping his head up so he could pass to teammates.

Larry's athleticism started to turn some heads, including Mr. O'Neil's. The math teacher was also a cross-country coach, and he was looking for new runners. He came up to Larry after a basketball game. It was always odd to see teachers outside of the classroom, but Mr. O'Neil was a good guy. Larry didn't mind it when the teacher greeted him outside the gym.

"Hey Larry," he said. "Saw you running out there; you're pretty fast."

Larry nodded.

"I'm looking for fast runners for the cross-country team, and I'd like you to come out for us," Mr. O'Neil said. "I think you'll be great at it. Just no fighting."

Mr. O'Neil chuckled and Larry knew the teacher had seen some of his more aggressive tactics on the court. Larry liked being scouted, though.

"How far do you guys run?" he asked.

Mr. O'Neil put his finger to his temple and a smile broadened across his face. "Well, Larry, how about you join us and find out how far you can go?"

During the spring and fall seasons, Larry trained with the cross-country team. It was simple training: They ran. It was so simple that it became second nature. When it was hot out, Larry ran with the team. When it was cold out, Larry ran with the team. When it was dark out, early in the morning, chilly, freezing, or a strong wind was blowing, Larry ran with the team. No matter what, Larry ran with the team. When friends came over to the house to visit, Larry's mum would talk to them about the sports Larry played. When they came to talk about cross-country, she would always say the same thing: "Larry runs like a deer." The sound of her saying it made Larry feel free.

He especially liked running in the rain. Whether they were on the track or running through town, the rain came down and kept them cool. He'd been out in the rain lots of times, but being out in the rain by choice to run a long distance gave him a feeling of invincibility. He knew that the elements weren't going to stop him and they didn't. The running made him faster on the basketball court and the baseball diamond. He could skate faster for longer periods of time on the hockey rink, too. Every part of him felt stronger. Even though he was not on the legendary Everett football teams, he felt like a force to be reckoned with.

The Swan Street Rats had never all gone to the same school, so it wasn't a big loss being at a different school from Paul, Ronnie, and the guys. Back when Larry was at the Devens for elementary school, Ronnie and his brothers had all been at parochial school anyway. It wasn't school that kept them together then, it was the park. Later on, it was the jobs they scrounged up together.

One of the guys in the neighborhood was Dante. When he was little, nobody noticed at first, but as he got older, people realized that Dante wasn't all there. He was a special-needs kid. His dad was a great guy, and a hard worker, but as Dante got older it was harder and harder to take care of him. By the time Larry was in tenth grade, Dante was practically was a grown man, but he could barely speak, much less read or write. He was a great guy, though.

The guys would meet up with him downtown and make sure he had groceries to bring home to his dad and that he came with them to get his hair cut. Ronnie and his brothers lived near him on Andrews Street, so they'd go down to the barbershop. The gang made sure that Dante was taken care of and part of the group. Mr. Aiosa even gave him a job at the market so he could stock shelves and make his own money. He was a part of the neighborhood, and from the time he was a kid to when he grew up, the guys in the neighborhood always looked after Dante. It was bad business to come into Everett and push him around just because he was a little different.

As they got older, Larry and the guys got together in the basement of the pool hall to hang out. It was like being at the park but away from the prying eyes of parents and the motorcycle cop. The only windows in the place were thin, ground-floor panes looking out onto the sidewalk. Ronnie was setting up for a shot when he saw Dante's sneakers out on the street shuffling along. Then he saw two other pairs of leather shoes come up around Dante. He ran over to the wall and looked up while Dante's shoes went rocking back and forth. He didn't need to see much more to know that two other guys pushing Dante around.

"They're roughing up Dante!" Ronnie called out.

The pool hall emptied so fast that the cue ball was still spinning on the felt when the entire gang of eight guys came up the stairs behind Dante. Nobody waited a second before pounding the other guys. Larry was still thin but made sure he was at the front of that charge. He connected his elbow on the biggest guy's head a few times. Dante stood in the center of a circle of Swan Street Rats. They straightened his ruffled collar and pushed the wallet that the bullies had been going after back into Dante's front pocket. The intruders were off and running up Broadway with a few hard hits upside their heads. Dante came back down into the pool hall and then Ronnie drove him home safe and sound at the end of the night.

For Larry, there was something irresistible about the opportunity to fight. Seeing the way everyone was there for Dante, and being a part of that, was reassuring.

The gang did more to help Dante besides beating the hell out of anyone who gave him a hard time. After a few years of working at the market, Dante got it into his head that he should have his own place. His dad thought that was a great idea, but there was no way Dante would be able to actually pull that off on his own. So the Swan Street Rats stepped up. Ronnie helped find a nice apartment looking out on Chelsea Square. They worked out a deal with the landlord and they all chipped in to pay for the place each month. Now, in addition to getting their hair cut together, Ronnie and his brothers would help Dante with his grocery shopping and make sure the place was all set up. A bonus feature of this arrangement was that the guys had a place to go hang out if they wanted to get out of their houses. They each got a chance to experience life away from home without actually moving out. Dante loved it, of course, because his new place was the party pad. He always had visits from a few guys stopping by to have a beer after work.

As different as it seemed, the basics were the same as they had always been. After everything they had been through together, the Swan Street Rats were showing that they could somehow become honest-to-God men. Whether or not they played by anyone else's rulebook, they definitely had their own, and they followed it religiously.

Helen Giordano was raising five foster kids. Larry and Ruthie were the eldest now. They helped the best they could, but they saw things unfold in familiar ways. The twins went back and forth between their real parents and Dean Street, just like Ruthie had. It was hard to watch their shocked young faces in the social worker's car as it pulled away from the house. It affected Larry in ways he couldn't explain. Seeing one kid leave confirmed that he was always a sliver of a chance away from being taken away. It affected Ruthie even more. Not only did she have the fear of being taken away, but she knew what happened on the other end when your real parents don't work out and you come back, and then it happens again and again. She saw it in the other kids and it made her angry. She lashed out by not talking to Larry or Mrs. Giordano. She would leave for days and stay at friends' houses. For Larry, his fists had only just started to get him into trouble.

The priests and chaperones stood like sentinels all around the outside of the dance floor. Church mothers kept the punch and cookies piled up on the back table. Seminary instructors stood watch to prevent any extra ingredients from making their way into students' cups. The gym floor was converted into a dark labyrinth of teenagers running, flirting, and standing awkwardly with their hands in their pockets. Further on, past the shoulders of kids watching on the perimeter, was a dark wood dance floor packed with students practicing a mixture of jitterbug moves and solo twisting. The music came from an old record player and consisted of dance songs carefully screened for acceptable lyrics. It played some current dance hits and, of course, a sprinkling of slow songs. Once "Duke of Earl" wound down, the next single would be fired up and "Baby, It's You" by the Shirelles would crackle on to the speakers.

The coupling up would start under the even more watchful eyes of a dozen adults carefully positioned around the room. Kids who got too close together were separated to have the prerequisite foot of space between them and allowed to continue swaying to the harmonies, but now with their eyes glancing sideways for the next warning or intervention. Throughout the night, the dance was filled with chatter, music, and bursts of laughter as shoulders were tapped on, notes were passed, and shy girls nodded their acceptance to dance requests from nervous boys.

Larry and Billy Carrigan came in later in the evening. Ronnie had driven the guys in his parents' black-and-yellow Ford Fairlane. He had been reluctant to come because he had just formed a band and spent most of his time either practicing songs or trying to get gigs; the Catholic Youth Organization dance wasn't much help for his musical career. He circled around the block to park the car while the other guys scoped out the scene and counted the army of adults on duty.

"It's like a prison dance," Billy snorted. By the time Larry and the gang had gotten to the punch table where one of the teachers, Mrs. Donovan, come over, waving and smiling. Larry froze and gave his best polite smile. She had been his kindergarten teacher and he always tried to be respectful around her, but she seemed to think of him as some shy little kid.

"Larry! Is that little Larry?" Mrs. Donovan called out. She ran over and looked him up and down. "Well, I remember when you were this big!" she laughed, holding her open palm at knee height. Without looking, Larry could already tell that the guys were grinning and holding in their laughter. Mrs. Donovan kept at it, though: "I remember when you were the littlest thing, and now look at you!"

Larry smiled and nodded. "Hello Mrs. Donovan …"

"Where's Ruthie? You always went everywhere with Ruthie."

Larry looked at the floor and moved away from the guys who were busy filling glasses with punch and doing their best impression of showing how tall Larry was in kindergarten. "Ruthie's around somewhere. We don't spend as much time together these days."

"That's a shame, but look at you now, so tall! What are you now, 14?"

"Fifteen, ma'am."

She tapped him on the shoulder. "Don't you 'Ma'am' me, Lawrence Gagnon. Are you at the high school now?"

"No … " he said, stopping himself from calling her 'Ma'am' again. Instead, he rubbed the back of his neck: "I'm at the trade school. Sheet metal."

"Good for you! I knew you'd grow up to be a handsome young man," she beamed, and for a moment it seemed like she'd pinch his cheek. Nearby, Billy laughed and pointed. Larry winced.

Mrs. Donovan waved her hand. "Never mind him. I just wanted to say hello to one of the best-behaved students I ever had. She must be so proud of you, Mrs. Giordano."

"Thank you," Larry said, now sidestepping in the opposite direction toward the guys. Ronnie had just shown up and was joining in the spectator sport of watching Larry squirm.

"Have a good time, Larry," Mrs. Donovan called out before turning to help the other chaperones fill the latest empty cookie tray. Larry nodded and strode back to his snickering friends.

"So …" Billy laughed. "How about it?"

"How about what?" Larry asked.

"You asking her to dance or what?"

"Watch it," Larry glared, his hand reaching for Billy's collar.

"Ease up, rooster," Ronnie hissed. "Here comes Monsignor Hartigan."

The three paused their antics while the long shadow of the Monsignor approached. His hands swayed at his sides, gently nudging crowds of students aside as his silver hair and dark-rimmed glasses passed beneath the dimmed gym lights.

"Good evening, gentlemen," he welcomed them formally, like an envoy from a hostile nation. With good reason, too: Larry's time at camp was still fresh in both of their minds, as were the sporadic fights on the nearby basketball courts. These boys, and Larry in particular, had a reputation as unreformable troublemakers. They weren't the kind of customers Monsignor Hartigan was pleased to see show up to the dances. However, these CYO events were open to almost everyone, and he wasn't about to start kicking young people out of church-sponsored activities for no real reason. When they showed up, though, he was there to give them a stern look and warn them to keep on the right side of his fair, but firm, temperament.

Larry's brief time at Camp Cedarcrest had taken place two years ago. The Monsignor wasn't without regret about kicking Larry out of camp. The boy could have clearly benefitted from time away from his neighborhood, time in God's nature. But at the end of the day, it had been all about the rules. The Monsignor lived by the written word, whether it was in the Bible or in the camp handbook.

Larry looked at him straight on, still numb from being kicked out of camp. He was consumed by an innate refusal to back down, even for a second, even at another place where this glaring, bespectacled man could kick him out. Larry's inner voice was just as stern as the Monsignor's glare: *Fine, kick me out again. See if I care.* He felt as though they were about to clash again. But not this time. Instead, Larry saw the Monsignor's open hand gesture toward his, and his stony face glinted with a hint of warmth.

"Larry, I hope you have a good time tonight." The Monsignor remained composed. They shook hands.

"Yes, sir," Larry said, returning his respect.

"And behave," the Monsignor concluded, his grip tightening. Then he smiled graciously at the other two boys to include them in the warning. They all replied with another "Yes, sir." The Monsignor turned and strode away through the swaying sea of students.

Billy whistled his low, impressed whistle. "You know, on second thought, you better not dance with Mrs. Donovan after all. Lay low."

"Shut up, Billy," Larry snapped, tapping a solid finger into his chest.

"Hey, lay off," Billy mumbled, but before he could get another jibe in, Larry darted off to the back of the gym. He took a place against the wall, letting his eyes adjust. Then he circled through the students at the edge of the dance floor. Each smiling face seemed alien to him. How many of *these* kids had been threatened with being thrown out? How many had been set up as slave labor at camp and then kicked out? He swallowed a rising gulp of anger and turned toward the doorway with a mind to leave. There, he saw Annabelle Ferris walk in.

Larry's eyes fixed on her long brown hair and green dress as she meandered into the gym with her friends, her head bopping lightly to the music. A glow encircled her from the party lights strung about, and their twinkling transformed her face continuously as Larry watched her explore the room. He was transfixed. She had always been a cute girl, but Larry's ability to talk to her had never gone past the quick exchange that came along with finding a seat in the Parlin School classrooms they had shared, or bumping into her at a football game. His baseline politeness was applied at those encounters, but he'd never really spoken to her, even though he always wanted to.

Now that she went to the high school, it seemed like he'd missed his chance. They'd both be out of school soon. It seemed impossible for him to ever have an opportunity like this again. Certainly not with her in a green dress and him in a tie with his clean Sunday jacket. For a few minutes, he watched the other boys talk to girls, to get the general idea of what he should do. Larry was more accustomed to chatting up girls from a porch in the neighborhood. He didn't know the script on this strange stage, crowded with performers and an audience.

These were all kids who had grown up together, Larry assumed. Their parents had known each other before their kids were even born. Sometimes a boy would walk up to a girl and just nod—and off they went. If they did talk, it was something easy like "How about it?" with a hooked arm open for the girl to accept. Larry knew he could do that; he was sure of it. But he couldn't *actually* go do it. He felt something inside stopping him, something that followed him around everywhere and whispered, *You don't even belong here. You're different.* He could almost hear someone calling him a state ward to add to his hesitation. He was a ghost haunting

Everett, passing through buildings, listening to people, but never belonging.

Ronnie and Billy found him there in the depths of the gym. They came up and grabbed him by the shoulder, speaking hurriedly about everything Larry had missed just then in the hallway. Their voices and friendship meant everything to him in that moment. They were his brothers and having them there encouraged Larry to believe that he could ask Annabelle to dance.

Billy didn't wait at all to dive into the proceedings. He leaned in toward the nearest pretty girl: "Hey Emily, I've got a dance with your name on it."

"Sure, Billy," she replied, walking toward the dance floor.

"No, not yet, wait until they play 'Teenage Idol,' that's my song," and he'd share a laugh with the girl before moving on to the next one.

Ronnie was with his girlfriend, Patty. When the two of them weren't dancing, he'd go up to girls and say, "Hey, if you've ever wanted to take your life in your own hands ... now's your chance. Dance with Billy." Ronnie also spent some time talking to the priests about what it would take for his band to play one of these dances. Negotiations didn't go as smoothly as he would have liked, but he was an eternal optimist, and always ready to play any venue.

Meanwhile, Larry was focused on finding Annabelle. The record player was starting up on the opening notes of a slow song, but he'd lost sight of her. He scanned the room hopefully.

"Who are you looking for?" Ronnie asked.

"Annabelle Ferris," Larry said.

"Oh yeah, she's around. There she is with Mikey."

Larry's heart dropped to his stomach. There she was, dancing with Mikey Pappalo, one of the kids from Glendale Square. His mousse-thickened hair was combed back, bouncing light off his head like a metal helmet. His hands were gripped around her waist, and the two rocked side to side with the music. Annabelle seemed settled, and Ronnie watched Larry's fists clench in the familiar way that had preceded all the fights they'd been in together.

"Whoa, whoa there, Larry," Ronnie said. "Just wait for a new song and ask to cut in, pal."

So Larry waited. Ronnie and Patty danced. Even Billy got a dance partner by treating a girl to his rendition of the Twist. It was completely off tempo because the band was playing a slow song, but the girl laughed and away they went to the dance floor where he kept trying to get too close and she laughed and shoved him back playfully while the chaperones edged nearer and nearer.

Larry watched and waited, and then the band stopped. He guided himself toward Annabelle, who was standing alone again. He waited a moment for her to turn and notice him. He looked at her, and a smile came to his lips as he started to speak: "Could I have the next da ..."

Before he could finish, Mikey tapped his shoulder: "We're all set, pal. How about you go get a cookie?"

Larry's blood instantly boiled and he snatched the wrist poking at his shoulder with an unexpected, ironclad grip, developed over a decade of swinging a sandlot bat. Mikey pulled away and both boys made fists, but Larry's height gave him a couple of inches above the other kids on the floor and an unmissable view of the cadre of priests and parents looking directly at the scuffle. They would have a clear view of Larry if he decided take a swing, so he dropped his fists and walked away.

At 10 o'clock, the lights came on and the music stopped. Larry grabbed Ronnie and Billy and guided them to the Fairlane before the other kids crowded out the door. Larry dropped his jacket in the back seat, rolled up his sleeves, and jumped in the car.

"Let's go. But keep us in view of the door," he said. Billy and Ronnie looked at each other, shrugged and got in. Ronnie started the engine.

Larry's arm dangled out the rolled down window, his fingers tapping the outside of the door impatiently. Mikey and Annabelle came out of the dance together.

"There they are," Larry said. "Follow them, Ronnie."

The couple walked hand-in-hand down Broadway to the edge of the church grounds. As their steps took them past the church to the downtown, Larry unlatched the car door and skipped out of the crawling vehicle. Ronnie and Billy realized what Larry was doing too late.

"Larry, wait!" Ronnie slammed on the breaks and opened the driver's side door, but Larry was already across the street and he wasn't listening anyway.

"Hey pal," Larry said, planting his foot half a pace in front of Mikey, who turned just in time to see Larry's stone-still face.

"Remember me?" Larry said as his arm circled back like a

wrecking ball. The stars in the cold night sky rotated overhead. Mikey moved to swing at Larry far too late. Larry's punch landed and the impact knocked Mikey off balance. Larry's anger drove him to another instantaneous choice. He could have grabbed the falling boy by his collar and held him in place, but he squared his shoulders and stepped forward again, pounding Mikey's open chest with a heavy open-handed shove that lifted the boy off his feet and directed him through a broad, shining shop window. Mikey's impact was followed by the sharp, crunch of a thousand shards of sheet glass.

Annabelle shrieked, and Larry paused to see stubborn bits of glass fall from the window frame down onto the stunned boy, who was lying half inside and half outside of the shattered shop window. Then came the sound of heavy feet running toward them. Larry ran back to the car and dove into the back seat. Ronnie didn't have to be asked to slam down on the gas. The revving of the motor was lost in a maelstrom of confusion. Each second was a different feeling. Larry regretted laying out Mikey like that. He wanted a few more swings. The three boys looked at each other in the passing glare of the streetlamps. The car took the first corner and then Billy took a deep breath.

"Larry, did you just kill that kid?"

Helen Giordano had felt the keen misfortune of a police detective knocking on her door before. That shock was nothing compared to the chaos that descended on Dean Street. It started the day after the dance when one of the priests from the Immaculate Conception came to the door and asked for Larry. Without knowing exactly why he was on her porch, Helen called Larry down to see a tall, thin priest with dark hair and an agitated look on his face. The priest fixed a steely gaze at Larry and spoke to him, in no uncertain terms.

"Larry, I'm banning you from all CYO activities."

Helen was shocked. Larry's reaction was irritation.

"Why?" He asked.

The priest described Larry punching Mikey Pappalo through the window.

"He deserved a smack upside the head," Larry said, "and he's lucky he didn't get more."

"He's lucky that he's not in the hospital," the priest replied.

"Lay off me," Larry snapped back.

The priest's eyes narrowed. "You need to know that your actions have consequences. For you, and for your foster mother."

"My mother," Larry corrected.

"For you and for her," the priest continued. "I've put a call in with the police."

Larry's rage went white hot. He seethed.

"Screw you! Screw you! I don't need your CYO, and go ahead and call the cops. I'm joining the service," and he walked off the porch, down the driveway and into the streets of Everett.

Behind him he left his mum, someone he cared the for more than anyone else in the world. He couldn't bring himself to face her. He couldn't own up to disappointing her like this. The social worker had told him that his father was in the service for a reason. Larry knew what he was going to do. He had toyed with the idea of working a regular job, staying in town, and being a part of the gang forever. He had wondered what it would be like to get an apartment in town, maybe save up for a house in the neighborhood. He wanted that. He didn't want to leave his mum or the guys.

This choice had been made for him, though.

Punching Mikey through the store window was a sign. He wasn't normal. They didn't want him at their camp. They didn't want him at their dance. They couldn't wait for him to mess up and steal a bike, or deck a kid who deserved it. They took every chance they got to point a finger at him and say, *We told you he was trouble. This is why nobody wanted him. This is why he was given up as a foster child.*

Did everyone want the cops taking him off to some juvenile court?

He wasn't going to let it happen. He was going into the service. He would be long gone to someplace far away. He imagined something from the movies: standing on a ship in the South China sea, watching the sun fall far beyond the horizon, 10,000 miles from anything. He'd breathe new air. He'd walk through strange cities that nobody in Everett would ever see. He could be anyone he wanted to be. Nobody would know he was a foster kid. It wouldn't matter if he had been left in a hotel room as a baby. This was a chance to be just like anyone else. This was his chance to find some place on the planet where people didn't cover their mouths and point at him because he didn't have parents.

Larry wanted that chance, so he went to the recruiting office.

Walking into the Air Force recruiter's office got him all sorts of advice about where to go and what to do. It wasn't unusual for guys to come in off the street looking to enlist. However, for Larry, it turned out that joining the service wasn't going to be easy. He hadn't graduated yet and needed approval from the trade school. Fortunately, his teachers and the guidance counselors were glad to recommend him for the service. It was a natural next step for someone studying sheet metal. That wasn't the problem.

Larry was only 17. In order to join a branch of the service, he needed his parents' consent. Fortunately, his mum agreed that it was the right step. She knew that he couldn't stick around and wait for the police to come talk to him about Mikey being punched through a window, or whatever the next thing happened to be. Larry had a well of anger inside of him that wasn't getting any better staying in Everett. Helen knew that he wanted to go and she was ready to help him. That wasn't the problem.

Mrs. Giordano wasn't Larry's legal guardian. The state was in charge of Larry. He needed to get permission from his social worker to join the Air Force. So, Larry found himself back in the small office belonging to Mrs. Gould, surrounded by stacks of papers on every side. Fortunately, she was more than happy to help Larry. In fact, she seemed extraordinarily pleased. Mrs. Gould credited herself with guiding Larry to this decision by sharing the information about the boy's father being in the service. Mrs. Gould was quick to contact the recruiter to start the process of enlisting Larry in the Air Force. That wasn't the problem.

The real problem was that once Larry had gotten permission from his teachers, and Mrs. Giordano, and all the social workers who filled out all of the forms ... the Air Force recruiter went through the pile of papers and said: "Now all we need is a birth certificate."

Most people don't think twice about having a birth certificate. When they can't find a copy of it, they ask their parents, or go down to the clerk's office in the town where they were born to pick it up. That is, if they know who their parents are, and if they know where they were born. Larry didn't know either of those things. The work of locating Larry's birth certificate was so difficult that even the social workers at the state's Division of Child Guardianship couldn't figure it out. When Larry's real mother had given birth to him 17 years before, the hospital had used her real last name and then given Larry that real last name on his birth certificate. Only two weeks later, Larry's mother had checked into a hotel in Springfield under the assumed name of Gagnon. So somehow Larry's name had been changed to that fake last name on all the paperwork. Even though everyone knew it was an alias, they couldn't track down the right birth certificate in the hospitals around Boston. As far as the officials in the United States government were concerned, there was no proof that Larry Gagnon existed at all. After all these years of wanting to be a Giordano, it turned out that Larry wasn't even a Gagnon.

The actual birth certificate was unearthed after weeks of searching through records in Boston City Hall. Mrs. Gould found one that matched the day and first name. It also matched up with the police reports from when Larry was abandoned. She showed the document to Larry before it was delivered to the Air Force. Nothing about it seemed familiar. His name at the top of the document was Lawrence Pelletier. He'd never seen that name before. The space for "mother" was filled in with another name he had never seen, "Marie Jean Pelletier."

"That's your birth mother's name," said Mrs. Gould.

Larry passed the document back to her.

"Where is she?"

"I don't know," said Mrs. Gould.

He looked past her. Larry was sure that somewhere among the stacks of papers in Mrs. Gould's office there must be some way to find his real mother. He could only assume that she didn't want to be found. After all, she had left him in a hotel room. He wanted to know why she did that. That question would have to wait, though. He was on the fast track to enlist.

Larry passed all of his exams and the Air Force formally accepted him. The birth certificate was filed with the rest of his documentation. All of this had taken so long that Larry was just a few weeks away from his 18th birthday. But it didn't matter, the date was set, and Larry was leaving for the Air Force. Not only that, but the Air Force legal department offered to do all the paperwork to get him a new official birth certificate. It would take a long time to finalize, but it could be done.

When Larry learned that, he thought about his birth mother's name on the old document. Then he thought about Dean Street and the strong, stern woman who had been looking after him for as long as he could remember. He wondered out loud to the legal officer: "If I get a new birth certificate, can I change my last name?"

Helen Giordano was no stranger to the feeling of saying goodbye to her children. She had seen her boys off to college and celebrated her daughter Clara's marriage to an Air Force officer who was now stationed in Turkey. Now that Larry had decided to join the service, and had an enlistment, she was surprised that she felt something completely different than she had before.

There was no relief in knowing that she had safely raised Larry from the age of three to 17. She didn't share the confidence of her friends who said that the Air Force would straighten Larry out. To her, he was straightened out; it was the rest of the world that warped him into something he wasn't. He was a good boy. She didn't want him to go, but if he had to go, she wanted to know that he would come back and show everyone what a noble young man he had become.

The little boy who had been brought to her for care was gone. They were going to put him in a uniform and take him to some distant corner of the world. To the social workers, this meant that Larry was no longer someone to monitor. But for Helen, the caring never ended.

She was happy that Larry would be safely out of town. He wouldn't be liable to get into any more fights. The priest had agreed not to press the shop window incident with the police because Larry was enlisting. When Larry came back, he would be prepared to get a job. He'd learn how to be strong and independent. These were all the good things, she thought. There was more to it than that.

Helen also realized she would never see him graduate from high school. She wouldn't see him go to prom. If he was gone for very long, she might not see him get married. All the years of worrying about his safety and trying to keep him out of trouble melted away to the fear of losing him forever. Suddenly, the permanence of Larry being a part of her house was revealed as an illusion. There was nothing concrete keeping them together as a family.

In the weeks leading up to Larry's departure, Mrs. Giordano got a phone call from one of Larry's social workers: "Mrs. Giordano, my name is Ruth Guerette. I'm a supervisor at the Department of Child Guardianship. I wanted to give you a call to go over a few things regarding Lawrence's enlistment."

"Of course. What can I help you with?"

"Well, Mrs. Giordano, this might be a bit of a delicate question, but it appears that Lawrence's birth certificate was never corrected to match the name he was given in our files. He has been enlisted in the Air Force using a provisional form so we can include the old birth certificate. None of that affects you, of course, but something came up the other day that I thought you should know about."

"What's that?"

"Well, the Air Force legal department sent a memo to Mrs. Gould, Lawrence's assigned social worker, offering to draft a new official birth certificate for him so his name would be consistent everywhere."

"Very well. Is that something I need to help with?" Helen asked.

"Not necessarily ... except." The voice on the other end of the line trailed off.

"Except what?"

"Larry asked if his permanent name could be Giordano."

Helen didn't reply. In her mind's eye, the room around her filled with the mud-tracked footprints of Larry's sneakers coming in from baseball at the park. She heard years' worth of echoing voices during mealtimes and doors slamming as Larry and Ruthie left the house every morning for school. She recalled the sight of Larry appearing in the side doorway for dinner. She let herself appreciate the effort she had gone through to put together a family and make Larry feel welcome, and that appreciation filled the house around her and lit memories in her imagination.

She had never been Larry's real mother, but now she knew he wanted her to be.

"Mrs. Giordano? Are you there?" came the voice on the phone.

"I'm here. You can note down that I would be very happy to allow Lawrence to change his last name to Giordano."

"Wonderful to hear, this isn't going to happen any time soon," Mrs. Guerette said, "But it will be helpful for us to include a note that you approve of the change in Larry's file if they are able to get to the change down the line."

"I understand," Helen said.

She rested the receiver back on the phone gently, processing what was the most pleasant phone call she had ever received from one of Larry's social workers.

"You know, I always liked your part of Dean Street, Larry. Mrs. G has a nice house too," Paul Amici mused while he sat on Larry's front porch with Ronnie and Billy. They each had a paper cup of punch and there was a plate of cookies out on the railing. Larry's mum had thrown him a going-away party. All the neighbors were inside the house, so Larry and the guys sat out on the porch talking things over.

"Yeah, I like it too," Larry replied.

"What are you going to miss the most, Larry?" asked Ronnie.

"I don't know. A lot of things, I guess."

"You going to miss old Mr. Grant down there?" Ronnie asked, pointing at the gray house down the street. Larry smiled and shook his head.

"What about Mr. Grant?" Paul asked.

"Larry stole his chickens!" Ronnie exclaimed, laughing at the memory.

"Shut up, that was a long time ago," Larry smiled. He remembered when he and Ruthie were little kids petting the baby chicks that Mr. Grant had in his yard.

"Didn't you also used to mess with his Easter eggs?" asked Billy.

"Every year," Larry casually recalled. "He put them out late the night before so I'd watch from here and then sneak over and hide them all in different places."

"You sure you're not going into the CIA?" joked Ronnie.

Larry shook his head and chuckled.

"Why'd you choose the Air Force anyway, Larry?" asked Billy.

"Clara's husband, Eddie, is in the Air Force," Larry said. He thought about it some more. "He seems like a great guy, so I figured I should join up in the same branch as him."

"You're gonna make a hell of a fighter pilot."

The side door swung open and Ruthie came out with Dolly from next door. She ignored the other guys and waved at Larry.

"There's the big-shot soldier himself," Ruthie smiled.

"How is it in there?" Larry asked.

"A lot of old women talking about a lot of meatloaf recipes," Ruthie rolled her eyes. "We're going across the street. See you after this all blows over."

Yeah, Larry thought, *but not for much longer*. Larry and Ruthie, the inseparable duo, were about to be separated. He wondered how she'd get along. She only had a few more months of school left. She could stay with Mum as long as she wanted, but who knew how long Ruthie could handle living here, being asked to help with the younger foster kids. Larry had to get out, so she must be feeling the pressure too, except she wasn't joining the Air Force to get her out of being a ward of the state.

The door swung open again. Out came some of the girls from school: Nelly, Annette, Nancy, Carol, and Shirley. They sat on the porch for a while and made small talk. Then they went across the street, too.

"I'm starting to think the real party is across the street with all those girls," said Paul.

"You guys can go, I'll stay here until it's over," said Larry.

"Alright, see you later, pal," Paul said. "Enjoy the punch."

The guys patted Larry on the back. Every time they saw each other now, there was a feeling that maybe this was the last time in a long while. Still, they weren't being sentimental about it. They figured Larry would be gone awhile, so would some of the other guys, and eventually they'd all be back together. Larry sat back down on the porch and wondered what he'd be like when he came back from the service. He pictured himself stepping off the trolley in a dress uniform and all the guys buying him a drink.

The next time the door opened, it was Benny. The two guys smiled at each other and shook hands.

"Ma's really happy," Benny said. "She's proud of you, Larry."

Larry didn't know what to say. "What do you think, Benny?" he asked.

"What? About you going into the Air Force?" Benny shook his head. "I always knew you were tough, kid. Go get 'em."

Larry smiled. Benny turned to walk out to his car, but stopped.

"Listen, Larry, as far as I'm concerned, we're always gonna be family. You understand?"

Larry nodded.

Benny nodded back, and trotted down to the curb. Larry watched him drive away. The porch was empty. An airplane flew low overhead, filling the air with that familiar dull roar. Larry looked up and down Dean Street and imagined what it would look like to someone flying overhead.

Less than a week later, Larry packed his things, said goodbye to his mum, and joined a dozen other recruits aboard a bus that took him to Logan Airport. The first plane ride Larry ever took was the one that took him to join the Air Force.

Helen Giordano (top) with the foster children she cared for,
including Ruthie (middle row, center) and Larry (front row, right)

Larry (front row, center) on the Everett Vocational High School
basketball team

Larry's enlistment photo (left)
Larry visiting The Alamo during Basic Military Training at
Lackland Air Force Base in San Antonio, Texas

Larry (center) at the fire station on Sembach Air Force base with
Joe Griffin (right), who inspired him to study karate

Larry wearing his Everett Vocational High School athletics jacket
in Germany during his enlistment in the Air Force

Larry on Sembach Air Force base during his deployment (above)
One of the trucks driven by the base's fire fighters (below)

Twenty-two weeks, Larry thought. Twenty-two long weeks of training had gone by. It had begun under the archway at Lackland Air Force Base in Texas, with the clear block letters that read, "Gateway to the Air Force." That was where he spent the first eight weeks for what everyone calls boot camp, but is actually named Basic Military Training (BMT).

It was a strict daily routine that laid other guys flat on their back, but it wasn't too bad for Larry. Getting up at 4:00 a.m. to the sound of a blaring trumpet to go on a five-mile jog through the cool Texas air wasn't that tough. He had done plenty of running in school, and he'd rather do it early before the sun came on strong in the middle of the day. The classes brought him up to speed on military procedure. He learned how to clean, assemble, and fire a gun. The other guys in his bunk were from all over the country. They were nicer to him than the guys at camp had been.

Then Larry had two weeks off to go home in his crisp military uniform. There was an unmistakable hint of pride in his mum's face seeing him come back to the house on Dean Street as a military man. The time home flew by. There was something nice about walking around the same town where the cops had been out to get him, knowing he was out of it. He knew he was on his way to a new adventure. When he got his assignment, it was a badge of pride.

"What are they having you do, Larry?" asked Ronnie.

"I'm going into the fire department," Larry laughed proudly.

The guys who had grown up together setting things on fire in Swan Street Park looked at each other and then looked back at Larry. They burst into laughter, shaking their heads in amazement.

Despite the irony, becoming a firefighter was a badge of honor for Larry. The firefighters in town were well-off by most standards and well-respected. The fire department in the Air Force was almost completely different, though. Larry quickly discovered that a pile of burning Christmas trees in the park was completely different from the tower of flames that could be ignited by containers of jet fuel. The fires at an Air Force base could be anything from a small car fire to an explosion of rocket fuel. Larry's assignment to the Air Force Fire Department made him a member of a special unit and thrust him into a world of danger that he never expected.

His next level of training took place at the Air Technical Training Center on Greenville Air Force Base in Mississippi. For 12 long weeks he worked in conditions that were hotter and more humid than Texas was. The coursework was rigorous and intense, as instructors drilled into each of the recruits a complex series of procedures that had to be followed for every possible scenario. By the end of the training, Larry had the technical skills necessary to be a structural firefighter. He knew more than he ever thought he'd know about how to protect a base from being destroyed by a fire, but he'd also learned how to rip the roof off a burning car to save someone stuck inside. Every piece of equipment he learned how to use was a responsibility that had been entrusted to him. He didn't know where he would end up, but he knew that when he got there he could very well find himself in a deadly situation surrounded by people who were counting on him to do his job right. So he learned everything he could. He kept his head down. He didn't get into trouble. By the end of it, he felt prepared.

From Greenville, Larry was deployed to Sembach Air Force Base in West Germany. The purpose of American bases in Germany at that time was simple. His commanding officer put it like this: "If the Russians decide to drop nukes, we're the first ones to fire them back. If the Russians decide to invade, we're the first ones to fight back." The United States was in the throes of the Cold War. Two years before, U.S. Marines had undertaken a raid on Soviet-friendly installations in Cuba. It had failed. Since then, the East and West had begun building tactical nuclear missile bases around the world. Sembach was one of the United States' prime pieces of property, and Larry was its newest resident.

The living quarters were thick, bunker-like buildings laid out on one side of the base. The tarmac was on the other. There were two quaint towns with shops, restaurants, bars, and normal houses on either side of the base along winding roads leading through pristine forests. Germans in the area were given specific times when they could harvest the fallen wood in the forests for winter fuel. During those times, they picked the forest completely clean; there was no rotting wood beneath the branches. It looked like a movie set or a painting. Larry's first rides through the surrounding towns reminded him of the drive down to the Cape with his mum and Ruthie. They were quiet roads. They seemed far too quiet to be only a couple of hundred miles away from the Soviet army.

The weather was generally cloudy and windy. It was a relief after the 105-degree days in Texas and Mississippi. Larry's assigned uniform included an Air Force jacket that had been loose around his shoulders when he got it in Texas, but over the course of training his shoulders had squared to fill it. His schedule became more relaxed at Sembach. Instead of training every day, he had four days on and two days off. The four days on didn't seem like they would be that difficult, until his first shift.

The alarm sounded in the fire barracks and the guys on shift responded. They had their gear on and the Unit Commander had them assigned and loaded into trucks. As the sirens wailed around him, Larry was pointed to the driver's side of one of the massive fire trucks. "Follow the other ones," the Commander yelled as three other trucks pulled out. Larry had learned enough not to question an officer, and he figured, *How hard could it be?* If Ronnie could drive, so could he. Seconds later, his foot was on the gas while the big engine lurched out onto the connecting road to the base's landing strip. It wasn't as easy as it looked.

"Twenty-two weeks," Larry thought, "and they never taught me how to drive one of these things." He was barreling down the runway, doing his best to stay calm and focused. Sending this truck into a ditch wasn't an option. In the back of his mind, he wondered how he had gone from not having a bike to gripping the gigantic steering wheel attached to a state-of-the-art military fire truck. He pressed his foot to the gas and kept pace with the others. The speedometer said 50 miles an hour … and kept going up. At 60 miles an hour, he was overtaking the others. Still, the speed increased. At 70 miles an hour, he was blowing past the other trucks. The truck maxed out at 80 miles an hour with the plume of black smoke appearing ahead and growing rapidly. They had arrived at the site of the fire. Everything that had ever happened to Larry flew out of his mind and into the hurricane-force wind battering past the open truck window. Now, he had to figure out how to stop. His feet pounded at the pedals but they didn't respond. One of these had to be the clutch. Even pressing the pedal that seemed to be the brake didn't slow the down the vehicle, instead it lurched in an angry roar and kept flying down the tarmac.

This was 18-year-old Larry from Everett, Massachusetts. He had barely driven a normal car, much less something like this multi-gear, 20-foot-long monstrosity. The other firefighters in the truck realized what was happening and gathered around him, shouting above the din of the engine. They used hand gestures to show him how to push down on one pedal, then the other pedal, while pressing down on the right pedals in order to slow the truck. Larry stayed focused and executed each move, slowing back to 70, 60, and 50 miles per hour, until it gradually came to a halt a safe distance from the blaze ahead. The fire was a horrific sight.

Larry stared through the big windshield at the wreckage. Glints of tangled chrome poked out from the charred debris that was barely recognizable through the black turrets of smoke pouring out from either side. Larry couldn't tell what it looked like now, but this had been a 75-foot-long reconnaissance plane. The Douglas RB-66 Destroyer was notoriously difficult to land safely on the shorter runways at Sembach. This one had spun out of control and only two members of the three-man crew had gotten out safely. The commander pointed to two open parachutes fluttering in the distance.

The EMT units were racing toward them through the flaming debris that had rained down after the fuselage had collapsed onto the runway, sending showers of sparks and shrapnel exploding out of the central wreckage. One man hadn't made it out.

Larry didn't have time to think about that. His training told him what to do, and the other guys in the unit were already in the thick of it. He joined them in pulling out the equipment, setting the hoses, and connecting them to the reserve of fire retardant spray on the truck. Barriers were set up around the site as the flames got closer and closer to the plane's fuel tank. More experienced members of his unit fired the chemical liquid used to target the base of the flames and try to choke them out before they reached the main fuel source.

They couldn't stop it, though. Their commander signaled for them to take cover. The fuel exploded in a white-hot blaze, and the remaining wreckage rolled pathetically on its side and burned out.

The rest of the day was spent cleaning up. Bulldozers came to scrape the mangled fuselage off the runway so more jets could land. Another member of the crew drove the fire truck back. He laughed along the way, showing Larry how to work the gears. Back at the barracks, Larry sat at the window, watching a series of jets circling and landing. He knew that at any moment he was on, that scene could be repeated. Four days on, two days off. It didn't seem so easy now.

The bunks were spaced wide and there were two men per room. They were nice rooms, with comfortable wooden furniture. The base itself had been built around a former Nazi base, but over the years, NATO and the U.S. had built and rebuilt around it for each new asset that was added. When new missile silos went in, there were more engineers' quarters. Before a new squadron arrived, additional barracks and hangars were built. The fire station didn't change, though. It was out from the way of the rest of the operations. The guys in his unit operated more like a family.

Except for his short stay at Camp Cedarcrest, Larry hadn't shared a room with anyone since he was a little kid. His roommate was an older guy named Joe Griffin, a quiet Master Sergeant with thinning hair and olive skin. He had a New Jersey accent that made Larry feel less self-conscious about his thick Boston accent. Joe got along great with everyone, but there was also a very palpable sense that nobody messed around with him. He had a quiet determination that Larry recognized.

Plus, Joe had been on the base for two years already, so he knew everything. Without acting like a teacher, he taught Larry how to get around and how to act depending on which part of the base they were in. Everyone saluted officers, but Joe knew which ones you could talk to. Everyone went into town, but Joe knew which cafés were the friendlies to the airmen. Joe knew where to get the best food, and he knew how to bring food back to the fire station from the mess hall so everyone could eat there and hang out. He also knew how to get the TV in the fire station to work so they could watch reruns of *Gunsmoke* and *I Love Lucy* playing on the local stations.

The most surprising thing about Joe was that he liked to keep working. Larry didn't get it at first. He figured it was best to work your share and then relax, but Joe was always busy.

"Listen kid, here's the truth," Joe said one day after a shift when he went on his way to work on the engine of an old jalopy they'd found at the back of a hangar. "The worst thing you can do here is nothing. You'll go crazy if you get bored. You always have to be doing something. Trust me."

It was more than working around the base, though. Joe was learning how to fight. Larry came in from a shift early on to find Joe practicing some kind of martial arts in the bunk. His bare feet gripped the floor as he held a square stance and let loose with a series of punches, kicks, and blocks. His fists struck nothing, but Larry could tell that if they did connect with something, or someone, they would do serious damage. He took a wide circle around as Joe's fists continued to fly, threw his stuff down beside his bunk, and watched for a while.

"What are you doing?" Larry asked.

Joe didn't reply at first. He finished a roundhouse kick and overhead block before pausing and then turning to Larry. "I'm practicing, kid. You gotta keep practicing to get good."

"How long have you been doing that stuff?"

"Since I got here two years ago. I could do this all day and it makes the time pass." Joe threw a towel around his neck and went to the showers.

The other options for passing time at the base were pretty basic. Larry had gotten good at driving the trucks and drag raced them against other guys down the sides of the runway. But it wasn't the kind of thing he'd want to do every day.

They could also go to the non-commissioned officers' club and get a beer and food for a few bucks. The club had some pinball machines and a TV set up, as well as a pool table. Going there felt a lot like going to the pool hall in Everett. He wasn't about to get into the same kind of fights there, and it cost money.

There was also the town. Larry and the guys picked up an old Volkswagen and kept it on base. They worked on it constantly to keep the dilapidated thing running so they could ride into town for the night. There were certain cafés that were nicer to the airmen than others. The men did their best to talk up the German girls. It was a good time, but again, it wasn't something he could do every day. He'd run out of money or get bored.

For a while it came down to good, classic fun. Larry joined pickup games of volleyball and basketball on the courts outside the fire station. The games could go on for hours, with guys leaving to go on duty and then coming back and rejoining the lineup. Larry had a great time at the games, but there was still something missing.

Joe's obsession with karate was different than any other sport Larry had seen. Joe worked at it every night, even when he was exhausted from a shift. Joe just kept getting better and better at it. He seemed to thrive on every move, and get stronger with every practice. Larry wanted to try it out. One day, they were hanging out at the station and Larry asked him.

"Where'd you learn how to do that karate stuff, Joe?" Larry asked.

Joe turned his head calmly, and smiled. "I thought you might be curious about that. There's an instructor who runs a dojo out of a bar in town. You can go there for classes, or you can wait until he runs one on the base."

"How often does he have the classes?" Larry asked.

"Who's asking? You thinking about giving it a try?" Joe asked back.

"Maybe. If you think I should," Larry said. He knew that Joe was the guy to talk to if you wanted to get anything done around there. He was also someone who wasn't going to talk your ear off with a lot of nonsense. If he said it was worth a try, it probably was.

"I think you'd be great at it. You've got the reach. You're pretty fast out there on the basketball court. You ever get into a fight?"

"Here and there," Larry said, clearing his throat.

"You win those fights?" Joe asked.

"As many as I could," Larry proudly responded. Joe didn't smile back this time.

"Well, this stuff isn't for that, kid. This stuff is for learning something else."

"What do you mean?" Larry scoffed. He figured the whole point was to get a good jab in the next time someone started a fight.

Joe leaned forward. "It's not about learning how to win your next fight out there." He pointed out the window to the world in general. Then he looked Larry square in the eyes and put a finger to his own temple. "It's about learning how to win the fight that goes on up here."

Larry let out a long breath. Joe raised his eyebrows and tapped his head as a sign that Larry should think about that. The two had spent enough time together for Joe to know something about his young roommate. He knew Larry had something behind him in the States that he hadn't figured out yet. And with most guys like Larry, it wasn't a problem with the world; it was a problem with what they wanted to do with their lives. It was a problem with the discipline they had in their head to get it done.

Being in the Air Force was a good first step. Larry had to be disciplined here if he didn't want to get his ass kicked by the Commanding Officer. But he couldn't be in the Air Force forever. Larry might not have realized that yet, but Joe did. He stood up and looked out the window.

"I'm going home next year, Larry. And when I do, there will be no 4 a.m. wakeup call. There will be no rules and regulations to follow. If I'm lucky, I'll get a job in town and I'll be able to take care of my family. Do you know who's going to help me succeed?"

"Who?"

"Nobody. Nobody but me."

Larry looked out the window as well and thought about that. Joe turned his chair around and sat in it backwards. His arms crossed and he rested his chin on his forearms.

"Guess who's going to help you succeed when you go home," he demanded.

"Nobody … but me," Larry echoed.

Joe nodded.

"Listen to me good. You asked me if going to this class is right for you and I don't know. All I know is that you feel like you can succeed when you can put your fist through a brick. You get me?"

Larry nodded. He liked the sound of that. All in all, he was pretty confident that he could do whatever he wanted at the base. He didn't know what he could do when he went back home. Joe was right. The only person he could rely on was himself, and he might as well make himself the best he could possibly be while he had the chance.

"So can I come to a class?" Larry asked.

Joe gave him a thumb's up. "As often as you want."

Larry sniffed. He looked out the window at the low horizon of gray clouds and the forest line. *What's the worst that could happen?* he thought. *I might* like it.

Norbert Fay was a wiry man in his early 40s with short, thin, black hair. He had a calm face and a thin nose that only betrayed an inner intensity when it flared in the split second before he delivered a kick or punch. He taught karate wherever and whenever he could. Classes started in Sembach, just outside the base. One of the barrooms let Norbert use its space twice a week. The students would come to class early and move all of the tables out of the way. Another two nights a week, the class was held in the gym on base. Norbert arrived promptly and watched his students enter the gym respectfully before he led the class. The remaining three nights a week didn't have a dedicated space available. Joe and the guys at the fire station took the trucks out of the garage so practice could take place there, with Norbert's staccato commands echoing through the rafters.

Wherever they ended up practicing, the format of each class was always the same. The students formed rows to practice each component of the martial art, and then broke off to hone a series of those moves choreographed together called a kata. Finally, there was sparring: a brief opportunity to put on pads and let the punches connect before cooling down at the end of a class.

The look and feel of shotokan is something balanced and elegant. A student's feet and hands move in rounded symmetrical shapes around a centered core. The men practicing moved like river reeds, rooted to their stance but bendable to counterattacks from invisible opponents. The class looked like the wind blowing through a field of tall grass. Each student was focused and seemed at peace. Each of them seemed like he could fight an army.

Larry felt at home from the moment he arrived.

The session lasted an hour and a half. During that time Norbert, whom the students called "Sensei," didn't say much. He wasn't barking orders like a drill instructor. He didn't take particular notice that it was Larry's first class. He was used to new people coming and equally used to people dropping out. His entire focus was on the moment. Larry watched him complete a move and then replicated it. If he got it right, Norbert nodded. If he was off, Norbert held out his hand to stop him and then pushed his body into the correct position, speaking good English with a German accent: "Elbow here. Shoulders square. Feet farther apart." His instructions would continue calmly until either the stance was correct or he felt that it was a good starting place and it was up to the student to "Keep practicing this." Then he would move on to another student.

The practice session felt like it was over too soon. Larry wanted to learn everything. He wanted to have the power behind his punches and kicks that he saw in the other students. He wanted to keep practicing until he mastered it.

He attended class four nights a week, and on the remaining nights he practiced with Joe. His movements got sharper. His kicks got faster. Muscle memory sent his body into action without the slightest hesitation, and, most importantly, his mind became clearer. Each practice began and ended with a moment of calm where he had time to breathe in the good energy of the life he wanted to build, and breathe out the bad energy of all the dangers he had overcome to get to this point. He could have been injured or killed with the stuff he pulled growing up. He could have hurt someone else. He could be in jail. But he wasn't. He was here now. And he was getting stronger by the day.

When Larry joined the Air Force, the Department of Child Guardianship had formally closed its file on him. The State of Massachusetts was no longer responsible for providing assistance to Helen Giordano to help feed, clothe, and educate Larry. They had sent signed letters from directors that were carbon copied and filed away to indicate that Larry's upbringing was formally, and officially, complete.

For Helen, the business of being a mother never formally or officially concluded. Now more than ever, she felt like Larry's mother. Larry's flight to Texas for training seemed like yesterday and his deployment in Germany felt like a long, cold night. She had no idea how he was.

The instructions for sending him letters were simple. She addressed the envelope, put it in the mailbox, and it was supposed to be sorted and arrive on the base within a month. It had been six months. Her Christmas card signed "Merry Christmas, Love, Mum" had gone out and Christmas had passed, and she had gotten no response.

She had visions of Larry fighting with the other airmen. Maybe he was placed in a holding cell on the base. Or worse yet, there was some kind of legal procedure going on and Larry was being condemned to a sentence. All of this was happening a world away and Helen had no hope for affecting it, or for comforting Larry while he went through it.

Helen had the benefit of neighbors and friends when Larry roamed through Everett. There were people who could say, "I saw Larry down at the baseball diamond," or "Larry's been hanging around that Fitch girl down the line." She had an idea of what was happening even when Larry was keeping a tight lid on what he told her. Now she was completely in the dark. But she didn't give up. She wrote a letter every week for 30 weeks.

The last thing she had heard from Larry was when the social worker had told her he wanted to take her last name. By God, if he felt like a Giordano, she was going to let him know he was a Giordano.

Larry was at the fire station. His mind wandered to karate practice. His fists clenched as he mentally practiced the motion of a forward kick followed by two quick punches. Joe had been right. This karate training had saved his life. There wasn't enough TV, beer, or girls in town to keep a guy from going crazy. He had found his groove, finally. After months of practice, he was getting good. He could see it in Norbert's reactions to his movements and he could feel it in the force of his back kick. The guy holding the bag when he kicked it had better get ready when Larry came up to practice. He was in for fast, focused power that sent more than a few sparring partners sprawling on their backs, dazed.

It had all snapped into place for him. He wasn't as angry at the world anymore. He wasn't as frustrated. He was hopeful somehow. It was as if he had found a hidden reserve of confidence in himself. Now he knew he would be able to do something. He was ready to take on the life he had been given.

The guys at the station called him "Bruiser" because working out seven nights a week on his karate had transformed Larry from a thin kid to a broad-shouldered powerhouse. When Thatcher and Dean from the unit had gotten leave to go on a road trip through Switzerland and France, they had convinced Larry to come along. "In case we run into trouble," they joked.

Fortunately, they didn't. Larry had enjoyed seeing Europe beyond the 20 miles around the base. The people had been friendly, and they had come from all walks of life. Whenever they stopped someplace in France, they heard stories of how half of the town had been destroyed during the war. He met kids his age who had no family left. He got the feeling that there was something more to life than scrapping and hustling enough to get by in Everett. He also got the feeling that some people out there were worse off than he was. They were happy and they'd been dealt a worse hand than he had. Larry appreciated his mum more than ever.

Now that he was in the Air Force, he was receiving a constant stream of letters from her. Sometimes he got two in a week if the mail doubled up. The notes inside were short, but they kept him from being homesick. He heard about Ruthie being a terror during her senior year of high school, and how the twins had been moved back to their real parents again. He heard about Clara's newborn baby and how she wanted Larry to come visit her and her husband while they were stationed in Turkey while Larry was nearby. The details about Thanksgiving and Christmas were pleasant reminders of all the good things about life at home, and each letter was a symbol of how much she really cared about him. He knew that on paper, she didn't have to do anything for him anymore. He was signed out of the system. But she still wrote.

And Larry didn't respond.

He had them all stacked up in his drawers, but he never wrote back. It seemed like she was more interested in sharing life in Everett, and that there wasn't much to say about life on the base, anyway. Or, at least, that there wasn't much that she needed to know about life on the base. Larry had grown up under Helen Giordano's wing. She had provided for him. In that moment, he couldn't imagine that she needed something back, or that he had anything to give. Larry imagined wrong.

The streets of Everett had not gone quiet. Helen worried about Ruthie. Her letters to Larry didn't let on how difficult it had been since he left. Ruthie had dropped out of school twice. She had a boyfriend that she went to live with. Helen couldn't find a way to bring her around.

She became desperate to know if Larry was doing well. She needed some kind of reassurance that she had been a good mother to the kids who had come to her. So, she kept reaching out. Somehow, she would get through. She had to.

Inside, she felt something breaking from the strain of it all. She was used to being the strong one for her children. She wasn't used to feeling like this, feeling like she couldn't make it through.

❖ ❖ ❖

Joe Griffin's enlistment came up a few days after Larry's 19th birthday.

"You're an old man now," Joe joked. "I guess my work here is done. I can go back to Jersey."

Larry laughed, watching Joe pack his duffel. When Joe came to his karate belt he held it up. "Check this out," he smiled. "It's my black belt."

Larry nodded; he had been there the night that Joe received it. The black belt exam included students from across the whole school. They helped test the candidate in mock attacks and sparring. Larry knew Joe had earned it. His technique was superb. He'd thrown Larry once or twice along the way, and Larry was a solid eight inches taller.

"You think you're going to get yours?" Joe asked.

"Maybe," Larry said. A twinkle in his eyes showed that he was definitely going to go for it. A black belt was a lot of work, but Larry was well on his way. He was helping teach the new students now, and it was a lot of fun for him to see a sergeant come to class, only to have the sensei instruct Larry to teach him the basics. Larry would look at his pupil and shrug, as if to say, "Guess I'm the guy in charge here."

"What's the first thing you're going to do when you get back?" Larry asked. "Anything special?"

"Yes," Joe said.

"What?"

"I don't like to talk about it, but … we're roomies," Joe sighed. He pulled a photo out from the lining of his jacket and handed it over. Larry looked at it in shock.

"This is your kid?"

The photo showed a beautiful, blue-eyed baby in the arms of a curly-haired woman leaning on a boardwalk bench overlooking a wide beach. Joe shrugged and nodded.

"Yeah, she was born in September."

"You're kidding! Why didn't you say anything?"

"I took my leave and saw her over Christmas. Now I'm going back for good. Nothing more to be said. It's my business, guy. And I guess it's yours too, now. Keep it under your hat."

Larry nodded.

Joe kept talking. "Listen, Larry, you do what it takes to get that black belt. You're damn good. Even if you can't get it here, get it when you get home."

"Sure," Larry agreed.

"You promise?" Joe insisted.

"You bet," Larry smiled. "Now, if you'd excuse me, I have to go get something."

Larry ran down to the NCO and picked up a handful of cigars. On the way back, he found Joe in the midst of a crowd of guys, handed the cigars to him, and shook his hand.

"Thanks for being a great roomie, Joe. And guess what, guys: This Joe's a dad!"

The crew erupted into applause. Joe punched Larry in the shoulder and put a cigar in his mouth, passing a few of the others out. They watched him hop into the bus, chattering to each other about how he didn't bother to tell them.

"He felt like it was his business," Larry said.

"You think you'll ever have kids, Larry?" asked Dean. His Georgia accent rolled out pleasantly. Larry shrugged his shoulders as if to say, "Who knows?" The first thought in his mind wasn't about himself and a family though.

The first thought he had was about his mum.

That would make her the grandmother to my kids, he thought.

And that's when the loudspeaker crackled to life.

"Airman Larry Gagnon, please report to Base Commander

Thompson's office."

The guys went quiet and looked around to find Larry. He stood up and moved to the door. The response was automatic, but inside he was wondering what the hell he could have done now.

Larry was shown into the Base Commander's headquarters. A series of folded flags from his previous commands were framed on the hallway leading into his office, which was modestly appointed with dark wood and shelves filled with framed photographs and model aircraft. There were two chairs in front of the Commander's desk. Larry stood in salute for a half a second before Thompson waved him over: "Sit down, airman."

"Yes, sir."

Commander Thompson was a weathered man with gray hair and deep, creased wrinkles running the length of his face. He had a long chin and deep-set eyes that were sometimes entirely hidden behind the glare of light off the thin-rimmed glasses he often wore for inspections. He didn't have those glasses on at the moment, so Larry could see the deep look of concern on his face.

"I've asked you here because of your foster mother."

Larry's mouth went dry. He returned the Commander's look of concern.

"You know how she's doing, don't you?"

Larry thought he did. He had been getting her letters. She was worried about Ruthie. Something must have happened for him to be called here.

"Is she alright, sir?"

"You're a real piece of work, airman. How often does she write you?"

Larry raised his eyebrows. "Every week, sir."

"Every week. And how many times have you written back?"

"I haven't, sir."

Thompson pinched the bridge of his nose and shook his head as if trying to eliminate a terrible thought from his mind. He whispered Larry's answer back to him, "You haven't." Then he leaned back and opened the side drawer of his desk. He pulled out a manila folder with some pages in it. The tab was marked "Giordano/Gagnon."

"Let me show you something, airman," he said, spreading the papers on the desk in front of Larry. He scanned them and saw words like "URGENT" and "PLEASE RESPOND." They were written in his mum's handwriting. "Do you know what it does to a mother to write to her son every week for a full year and get no response?"

"No, sir."

"It drives her nuts, airman!" He shoved the papers into Larry's lap. "You're driving her nuts and she's writing letters to me now, and that's driving *me* nuts."

Larry read the letter to the Commander. "I'm writing to request information as to the well-being of Lawrence Gagnon. I have not heard from him since he was stationed there and have grown to fear for his safety after six months without a reply to my frequent letters …"

"That one was from six months ago," Commander Thompson seethed. "Stupid me. I thought you'd realize you need to write her back on your own. She just wrote this one, and she copied General Sinclair in Washington. So now by boss and I both know you don't know how to write your mother a letter. Can you read and write, airman?"

"Yes, sir."

"Not if these letters have anything to say about it."

The Commander slammed a fist on his desk and then reached into another drawer and pulled out a piece of paper and an envelope.

"Airman, I'm going to watch you write a letter to your mother right now. You will tell her you are healthy and alive. Do you understand?"

"Yes, sir."

Commander Thompson waved his hand as if to say, "Get on with it." Larry picked up the pen and wrote:

Dear Mum, Sorry I have not written sooner. I am alive and well here at the base. Thank you for your letters.

"Now promise you will respond to all of her letters from now on."

I will respond to your letters.

"I said ALL of her letters, airman."

All of your letters.

"Now thank her again for writing so often."

121

Thank you again for writing so often.

"And tell her she's a great mother."

"Sir, you should know she's not my real mother."

Commander Thompson's eyes almost popped out of his head. He slammed his fist on the desk again. "Airman, you listen to me. This woman raised you, correct?"

"Yes, sir."

"And she kept you out of trouble long enough to join the Air Force, correct?"

"Yes, sir."

"And she has written you for a whole year without getting a response, correct?"

"Yes, sir."

"Well let me tell you something then, airman. That makes her a good mother. PERIOD."

Larry nodded and kept writing.

Thank you for being a great mother.

"Now sign it and get out of my office."

"Yes, sir."

Larry signed his name, stood, saluted, and turned to leave.

"If I get one more letter from this woman saying you haven't written, you're going to be cleaning the length of that runway with a cotton ball for the rest of your enlistment, airman. Understood?"

"Understood, sir."

"Out!" The Commander said, pointing to the door. Larry walked out with an extra urgency, like a hive of bees had been emptied into the office. When he was gone, Commander Thompson folded Larry's letter, put it in the envelope, addressed it to Helen Giordano at 60 Dean Street, Everett, Mass. and put it in his outgoing mail pile. Then he leaned back in his swivel chair and let out a long sigh of relief, whispering to himself: "Damn kids."

Larry's enlistment ended in the summer of 1967. By then he had reached brown-belt level in shotokan. Norbert continued to be impressed by Larry's ability to master techniques. Larry was clearly ready to take a black belt exam, but the school at the base wasn't thriving, as it had been when Larry had started. Sensei Fay felt that Larry needed a new challenge and to be truly tested in order to earn his black belt. He felt there weren't enough capable high-level students at the base to put Larry through the exam.

Instead, the sensei recommended Larry look into a newly formed school called kyokushin. He had a sense that Larry would thrive in a more direct style that let his long arms drive opponents back, and one that let him actually attack an opponent with full contact. Norbert could tell that the core of Larry's success in martial arts was self-improvement and discipline. Those traits were said to be at the core of kyokushin.

Larry took the recommendation to heart, and took every opportunity to learn more about the style, something that took time since the school had only just begun. Rather than be frustrated, though, he kept working. The lessons he had learned from Norbert never left him. He knew that his training could take place anywhere, and that it was dependent only on himself and his own commitment. His core of self-discipline had grown from an acorn at the center of his military experience into an oak tree under the nourishing light of the basement dojo where he spent so many nights honing his abilities and dedicating his time to the rhythmic freedom of this newfound art form. Larry's goals for karate went beyond getting a black belt. He knew he would someday; he had made that promise to Joe.

He'd also made a promise to write to his mum, which he hadn't forgotten. She had been so relieved that he was alive and well that her letters came more infrequently now, and they were less frantic. After each one, Larry responded. As the time of his enlistment wound down, she started writing about getting his room ready for him. She wanted him to come back.

The letters painted a picture of the same bedroom with the same furnishings, the same football team photo with Benny at the center. Larry pictured life there and daydreamed of days at the park, nights at the pool hall, and daytrips to Revere Beach.

Larry had always known that his mum was willing to let him live on Dean Street again, but now he felt like she wanted him there. It buoyed his spirits to know he was coming home to the life he loved, and that he had left behind all the anger and fear he had felt growing up. Nobody could take him away from Dean Street now. It was only Larry and his mum, no social workers. Now, if it was time for Larry to get a new suit, he would go out and buy it himself. And he'd get something for his mum, too.

The new plan was simple. He was going to live at home, get a job, and save up money to start his own life somewhere. And one more thing: He was returning as a Giordano.

When the paperwork came through, Larry went to the NCO late at night so that he could telephone his mum in the afternoon with the time difference. He dialed the number and held the receiver to his ear with one hand. He held the revised birth certificate in the other. The text listed Larry's full name as "Lawrence F. Giordano."

"Hello?"

"Hi Mum, it's me!"

"Larry, is that you? The connection is so soft."

Larry spoke up louder. "Mum, I'm calling to introduce myself."

"Introduce yourself? What do you mean, Larry?"

"My name is Larry Giordano. Pleased to meet you."

The line went quiet and Larry wondered what she thought. She had told him it was what she wanted too, but he wished he could see her face to know for sure.

If he saw her in that moment, he would have seen her standing at the bureau with the phone resting on her chest and her hands brushing escaping tears from the corners of her eyes. She took a deep breath and picked up the receiver to speak.

"You were always a member of the family, Larry."

"I know, I know. I want you to know what it means to me."

His head filled with the images he remembered from the photo albums. Beside photos of his mum with Benny and Clara were photos of himself and Ruthie. Larry decided that his life started when he was three, and he was coming home.

Larry arrived back in Everett during the hottest days of summer. He got off his flight at Logan to be greeted by his mum and Benny. The homecoming felt comfortable and Helen offered to throw him a welcome-home party. Larry waved it off.

"All I want to do is get a job," Larry said.

He did three things right off the bat. First, he put his Air Force pay in the same bank account that his mum had set up for him to deposit his grocery-delivery money. Second, he got a job at a corner gas station. And third, he went down to the park and talked to some of the younger kids about learning karate. He was surprised at how many of the kids were interested.

He started by showing them the basics of a strong stance and a fast punch. Then, he began getting into the daily drills. They practiced each move carefully and he taught them their first kata. He realized he needed a space to really start teaching. His mum offered him the attic on Dean Street, and that's where Larry started his own karate school, "The School of the Rooster."

In no time, he had the gas station job, bought a white Thunderbird convertible, and he had started his own karate school. Larry felt like it was a whole different world. He was more free now than he had ever been and had a steady stream of money. He picked up shifts at the General Electric plant, sweeping up the machine-room floors and walking the security beat. On top of those jobs, he still had time to head down to the gas station and pick up an afternoon shift from Carl. After a few months, Larry came to look at that job as a nice way to spend the afternoon. Carl became more of a friend than a boss.

That was a good thing, too, because Larry spent most of his shift taking care of his car. The motor that raised and lowered the convertible roof was a nightmare. He and Carl would spend hours working on it, only to hit the button and see the roof shudder to a stop halfway between being up and down. They would spit and curse at the car before rolling up their sleeves and getting back to work. The repair attempts went on for months. Carl's wife Marilyn would come over to the station to find Larry and Carl in the garage surrounded by the disassembled parts of the car's roof mechanism.

"Well, well, well, if it isn't the wonder mechanics," she would laugh.

"One of these days we'll get it to work, Marilyn," Carl said.

"And when you do, Larry will end up owing you money for the time you spent working on the thing," she joked.

Eventually the roof motor worked, but that just freed Larry to spend more time spiffing up the rest of the car. He and Carl would yell at each other across the lot.

"Hey Larry, do you mind taking a break from polishing your own car so you could maybe take care of a customer or two? This is a business, you know."

"Relax, Carl, I'm on my lunch break," Larry assured.

"It's been three hours, Larry. You haven't moved an inch."

"I get hungry."

Larry did get a lot of work done, but he was mostly focused on standing out on that curb with his sleeves rolled up showing off for the ladies. Carl and Marilyn were always on the lookout to set up Larry with a girl so he'd settle down.

"How about her, Larry?" Carl said. "She looks like your type."

"Reminds me too much of Sally," Larry said.

"Sally, which one was she again?"

Larry thought about the brunette who had come by the station for a tire rotation. He'd talked her into a couple of date nights in Revere. They hadn't hit it off that well, though, at least not enough to keep on seeing her.

"Driving a girl out to Revere to watch submarines does not count as a date, buddy," Carl joked, shoving his shoulder. "We gotta find you a nice girl to make an honest man out of you."

"Good luck with that," Larry smiled.

The Flamingo Lounge in Saugus was the kind of place Larry would never have imagined going when he was a teenager. First of all, Saugus was a longer ride up Route 1 than any of the guys were used to. Even stranger was the decor. The seats were upholstered in a moody red velvet, and each table had a telephone on it, with a phone number up above it in big bold numbers. The blue walls reflected a soft wall of light as the bar filled with onlookers and groups of guys found their way to their tables while casually checking out the ladies in the place, and remembering the temporary phone numbers of whomever they found attractive.

The little restaurant looked like the cast of *Gilligan's Island* decorated it. Ronnie and Sonny Rocco had convinced Larry to go to this place. Ronnie had a steady girl, but he was always up to joining the guys on a night out. Ronnie's band was taking off and he was eager to get a sense of what people liked to dance to. He'd hang out anywhere with a jukebox. Larry wore a suit and tie; Ronnie rolled up his jacket sleeves and loosened his tie. Sonny had a jacket on but no tie. He had come from the old school of chatting up girls downtown and going to drive-in movies. He joked it would be good to see how the other half dates. Larry figured he was there for the drinks and the food. He didn't expect to get anything out of it but a fun night with the guys when he drove them there in the Thunderbird.

"You want to date that bird?" Ronnie asked, hopping out of the convertible and pointing up at the brightly flashing sign, bursting with tropical colors and featuring a cartoonish flamingo holding a telephone. Larry rolled his eyes. It was great to be back with the guys again. Whatever they were getting themselves into tonight, he knew it would make a good story later on. Especially if he could call up Sonny from another table and get into a yelling match over the phone. The last thing Larry expected was for this night to change his life forever.

"This place is nuts!" exclaimed Sonny.

"It sure is," agreed a mesmerized Ronnie.

"Well, let's hope the food is good," Larry declared. He smoothed his tie into his jacket as they made their way to a booth on the side of the restaurant farthest from the front door. Their table's phone number read #4. Larry made sure he had a clear view of the exit in case he needed to bolt. Ronnie pointed his thumb at a table of jokers in the corner, none of whom looked a day over 16.

"Looks like they got a kids' table," said Ronnie. "I didn't know school groups were allowed to order cocktails."

Sure enough, the waitress brought a tray of Mai Tais to the kids' table. She set them down and the boys and girls started sipping before an irate manager burst out of the back room, shouting at the waitress.

"Ah, young love," Ronnie sighed as the kids were swiftly ushered out of the building. The manager came back in and shook his finger at the waitress. By the time she came over to Larry, Sonny, and Ronnie's table, she was eager to ask anything that moved to show an ID.

"ID's, please."

"I'm turning 67 tomorrow, can I get a senior discount?" Ronnie asked.

"As long as you're 21 you get to stay," the waitress shot back.

"Fair enough," said Ronnie. "While you're here, can you get them to play 'Walk Away Renée?'" Ronnie had fallen in love with the song as soon as it came out. The waitress ignored him and took their drink orders.

"You might be the only one here addicted to that band," said Sonny. "What are they called again? The Right Tank?"

Ronne pointed at his friend. "They're called The Left Banke, pal. Remember it."

"Go put it on," Larry said. "There's a jukebox over there. People will go wild for it."

Ronnie didn't need to be asked twice. He skipped his way over to the jukebox and started an intense conversation with another music fan. Sonny shook his head and turned to Larry.

"You're dressed to impress tonight, my friend," he mused. "Just don't get any stains on your shirt before she gets here."

"Who?"

"Your girl," Sonny said, taking the serious tone of a fortune teller. "Your one and only."

"Well, when she gets here I hope she's carrying a cheeseburger," Larry chuckled. "I'm starving."

Over in the corner, Ronnie was getting into a heated discussion about The Kinks versus The Stones. Larry didn't care what music was on, but the place was starting to get going. People were hitting the dance floor. Ronnie was back at the table in a flash.

"This place is pretty damn nice, if you ask me," he said.

The front door opened and the first newcomer in was a shyly smiling girl with a glamorous, full hairdo and a long red dress with shimmer. Her dark eyes scanned the room amid the bustling dance floor. Larry kept his eyes on her as she looked through the throngs for a table. There was a simple, beautiful feeling that warmed his heart and set it beating faster.

Sonny noticed Larry's attention was focused somewhere and turned to see who he was looking at. When Sonny saw her, he poked Ronnie.

"That's it! That's her!"

"Who's what? Who's who?" Ronnie asked, dropping the food menu to see what he missed.

Sonny pointed in the general direction of the girl in the red dress. The way the room parted to let her through to a table made it clear.

"Oh wow!" Ronnie exclaimed.

Larry wasn't about to tell them to shut up. He was focused on what was happening in front of him. The girl kept looking around the room, and Larry kept looking after her, hoping for a moment of eye contact.

"Who's she here with?" asked Sonny.

The group in front of them had six other girls.

"That's a lot of beautiful!" said Ronnie. "Looks like she's got a gang of her own."

Larry looked over at Ronnie and nodded approvingly as if to say, "Good for her." Then he went back to figuring out which table she was going to sit at. The girl in the red dress and her friends were only occasionally visible through the moving dancers. Eventually, he decided to stand up to see.

"No Larry, don't stand up!" Sonny caught him by the sleeve. "Ronnie, you stand up, or dance over there and see what their phone number is."

"What?" Ronnie asked. "Why?"

"We want Larry to look cool and aloof," Sonny said. "Girls love that."

Larry stayed in his seat for another moment, but he couldn't sit still for long.

"Forget that, I'm getting her number myself."

Larry feigned walking toward the bar and passed through the tables on the other side of the restaurant. He saw her. She looked up; did she look at him? He couldn't tell. All he could do was get a look at the sign on her table that read #2. He dashed back to the guys.

"It's number two," he said. Before they could grab the phone, Larry picked it up and dialed the number.

While the phone rang, Sonny turned to Ronnie. "I hope you appreciate that we're watching a romance being born."

"Shut up," Larry snapped as the girls picked up on their end of the line.

There was a brief pause while Larry collected his thoughts. The dancers cleared the floor enough for him to see the girl holding the phone at table number two. It was one of her friends.

"Hello, you know that lovely young lady in the red dress you're sitting with?" he asked. "I would like to dance with her."

Larry watched as the girl who had the phone passed it to her dark-haired friend. She whispered something to her and everyone at table #2 cupped their hands over their mouths laughing.

The girl in the red dress raised the receiver to her ear and Larry heard a soft voice on the other side said: "If you want to dance, you're going to have to come over and ask me in person."

"I'll be right over," Larry said, beaming and giving a low thumb's up to the guys.

"How will I know it's you?" she asked.

"I'm just a clean-cut American boy," Larry replied, and with that he got up and walked straight to her table. Every step felt like a slow introduction. Along the way they made eye contact. He tried to shift his gaze confidently, but it always came back to her. It only took a few steps for Larry to be standing beside her table.

She looked up at him. He looked down at her. The fluttering in both their hearts fanned the room as Larry held out his hand.

"Hello, my name is Larry," he said. "Would you like to dance?"

"Eileen," she said as she took his hand and they went out on the floor together. Ronnie and Sonny watched from the booth.

"There it is, Ronnie," Sonny said.

"There's what?" Ronnie asked.

They watched for a while, and Ronnie tilted his head to one side as if to agree that something special was happening. Larry didn't come back to the table until the end of the evening. And when he did come back, it was with her phone number. That number led to long, pleasant phone calls and a first date. Then a second date. They became inseparable. Larry brought Eileen home to meet his mum. Helen loved Eileen like a daughter, and Larry worked hard to win the approval of Eileen's family over a string of beautiful days driving north to her home in Methuen. A year and a half later, the two visitors to the Flamingo Lounge were married.

Helen Giordano wore a blue dress to Larry's wedding. Benny Giordano was the best man. Eileen walked down the aisle in an intricate, embroidered white dress with a long, flowing veil. The dancing at the reception went into the late hours of the night, and in the midst of it all, Larry found himself sitting outside with Benny.

When he looked at Benny, he saw the closest thing to an older brother or father he would ever have. He looked at Benny and saw the guy who was always there for him growing up, the guy who had never missed one of his junior high school football games. What

Larry didn't know was how much he had meant to Benny and his brothers and sisters.

"Listen, Larry," Benny said. "I want you to know, and I mean this: I am so happy you changed your name."

Larry turned his head to one side. He had worried that Benny and Clara might have been offended by the name change. As he got older, Larry noticed how the kids in other families got territorial around their parents, even with their real brothers and sisters. Despite everything they had been through, Larry was still a foster child who had shown up at his mum's house after she had already raised her kids. As far as they were concerned, he could be a Johnny-come-lately—a newcomer who gave their mother hell for 14 years and then joined the Air Force. Then, he came back from Germany and suddenly he's a Giordano?

Benny could see what Larry was thinking and put a hand on his shoulder. "When Mom needed you, you were there. I watched her today and she saw you get married and she had the same pride on her face as when I got married."

"You're her son," Larry said, "I'm her foster son."

Benny took a swig from his beer bottle. "Do you remember when you got snagged for bashing parking meters? You must have been seven."

Larry thought back to it and nodded that he remembered.

"She called me that day and asked me to come over and talk to you. Did you know that?"

Larry knew Benny had come over, but he didn't know why.

"While you were tied up in the hallway she had me in the kitchen and do you know what she told me? She told me, 'Go in there and make him feel like he's a part of this family.' And I asked her, because I was just a kid myself you know, I asked her how I was supposed to do that. She looked at me with that dead serious look she has—you know the one—and she says, 'Talk to him the way you would want your older brother to talk to you.'"

Larry smiled.

"So that's what I tried to do," Benny laughed.

"You did good."

"Well I got that right, at least. You know we could have done without all the visits from the cops and punching kids all the time."

Larry took a sip of his beer and looked up at Benny.

"I guess I'm an exciting little brother to have around."

They clinked their bottles and went back to the reception.

Inside, Carl and Marilyn were talking about their latest competitive roller-skating moves. Since Larry had come back from the service, Carl had become like another older brother to him. They had spent holidays together. He and Eileen had gotten used to having them around for dinner, or going out places together on double dates.

The reception was a boisterous affair. Benny gave a wonderful toast. Larry danced with his mum. He danced with Eileen. He saw his family laughing alongside Eileen's family and he felt something he had never felt before. He felt like he could be complete, like he had everything he needed. There would always be part of him that wondered about his real parents, but it would be a curiosity, not a longing. He had a real mother; her name was Helen Giordano. After he got married and started his own branch of the Giordano family, Larry never felt like he had to question his place in the family again.

Business at Carl's gas station was booming, but it wasn't busy enough to start taking care of a family. Larry and Eileen lived in an apartment in Methuen next to Eileen's family for the next few years while they decided where to settle down. Larry upped his shifts at the GE plant and renewed his focus on karate. Since he had started taking classes seven years ago from Norbert Faye, Larry had trained constantly. During that time he had developed his own sense of martial arts and movement. He finally felt ready to seek out a school that taught the full-contact kyokushin.

The most prominent instructor was Sensei Steve Senne of Burbank, California. Larry flew out to train with him in 1970. He spent weeks observing and practicing techniques. He picked up on the core skills quickly, and impressed Sensei Senne so much that he tested for his first dan, or black belt, in kyokushin. That promise to Joe was about to be fulfilled. Larry had to demonstrate basic movements, performing kata, sparring, and tameshiwari brick breaking. They were all skills that Larry had begun to master in Germany; his continued practice at home in Methuen had given him the confidence he needed. Achieving a dan in kyokushin also required sustained combat called kumite. The minimum required rounds of fighting, or beating back repeated attackers, is ten. In a strange room, facing fighters he had only known for a few days, and far away from his family, Larry fought nonstop for an hour and half and passed. He became a black belt.

The achievement was so impressive to Sensei Senne that he recommended Larry go see Sensei Donald I. Buck in San Francisco. Larry met with Sensei Buck and continued his training. When he came back to Massachusetts, his sense of purpose was clear. His karate school became a central focus. He was one of a few instructors in New England, and as he grew his school, he started to receive invitations to tournaments. These were full-contact martial arts tournaments. Larry knew that these were the kinds of challenges he would have to face to continue to improve his skills in kyokoshin. He went to these tournaments knowing that the opponents wouldn't pull any punches. Neither did Larry.

Larry began traveling to fights with some of his advanced students. They would take road trips up and down the coast for a day of bare-knuckle rounds. With each win, the School of the Rooster gained more notoriety. It became clear to him that the next step in his career was to increase the difficulty of the fights. He attended more interdisciplinary tournaments and expanded his methods of attack so he could continue winning.

The most difficult tournament was held in a business basement in Boston's Chinatown. It was a full-contact, no pads, multi-round tournament. The only way to win was to knock the opponent out so he stayed down. Eileen was pregnant with their first child. Larry knew the danger involved, but he had a reputation in the region to build. He went for it.

It was a dark autumn afternoon with a heavy wind battering their windshield as Larry and Eileen drove to the tournament together. She had seen him fight dozens of times. He hadn't lost yet. Now, with their baby coming in less than a month, she was praying for his safety. This was the kind of fight where the people watching couldn't interfere, and it would be embarrassing for her to even speak if something went wrong. If Larry got into trouble, he was on his own.

The two schools met for the tournament and made customary formal greetings. The spectators took their seats around a square mat about 16 feet on each side. The participants sat cross-legged along each edge. When a round began, the instructor for each school would choose a fighter to go in. Larry's students were advancing quickly. Many of them were tough Everett kids like he had been, but they weren't all up to the task of facing hardened fighters in the ring yet. Larry started the tournament by selecting himself. He limbered his tall frame and walked onto the mat, preparing himself for his attacker. As expected, the instructor of the opposing Revere school stepped forward to face him. They bowed and began.

The rush of adrenaline that accompanied every fight washed over both fighters. Larry's mind emptied. The calm center of his soul took over, and he acted with the instinct of his training filling the void that decades of anger and frustration had left in his mind. The greatest lessons he had learned were all in evidence in that room. His wife and their unborn child represented the future. The karate school with his students represented discipline. His fists held firm with an attacker before him represented the challenges of a long life ahead. As his opponent's fists and shins crashed against the wall of blocks Larry put up, the last vestiges of a past that held him back evaporated from his reality.

A punch landed squarely in his chest. Another fist uppercut through Larry's jaw. Larry fell through the stories of his past and landed with a bloody crash. Eileen clasped her hands together tightly, guarding her body and locking her jaw to keep from screaming.

The attacker stood over Larry and noticed him moving and shaking his head to clear the fog of dizziness. There was an eternity of space between them, but a solidity of purpose in both fighters' eyes. Larry could feel Eileen's stare as he arched his back to throw his body upright. He could sense the kick coming in for his head. He rolled his shoulder to open up the space so the offending heel would breeze over him and then straightened himself into a tiger's crouch. His long arms were done blocking and they burst forward in a barrage of punches that pounded the wind out of the Revere instructor and sent him reeling. Larry feigned a kick to see his enemy duck and swung his heavy fist against the side of the enemy's face. The opponent's body went limp before it landed. The fight was over.

Larry waited to nurse his cut lip. The encounter was over. The instructors had fought each other in the first and last round. Larry bowed to the other school, and his students walked him and his wife out into the night. Winning the fight had meant a lot. Winning it calmly and having Eileen watching him win it that skillfully … that had meant everything.

In that calm center of a storm, they found their true strength. The world was now an unlocked safe. He and Eileen knew that they could set any goal they wanted, and together they could achieve it.

Eileen and Larry shared a love for family as the center of life. Their marriage and the natural movement of people moving to other states changed the nature of their family time over the years. The most immediate change was that the next generation of Giordanos swept into their world. Larry and Eileen had a daughter named Marie Jean, and two sons, Lonnie and Stephen.

Some of Helen's children moved away, like Billy and Clara. Others came closer and settled down within easy driving distance. When Larry and Eileen got together with Rosemary's family, they had a real crowd on their hands. Rosemary had married an engineer named Len. The two had eight children—Christine, Mark, John, Daniel, Julia, Andrew, Ellen, and Joel. The children called Helen "Manana," which was a combination of "my" and "Nana." Larry and Eileen enjoyed every opportunity to get the family together, hosting big barbecues and sitting out on the porch while all of the kids ran around the yard. Benny was always sure to be there, too. One of those family barbecues would change Larry's life direction yet again. Benny needed help.

"Listen, Larry, you know a lot of people up there in Methuen," Benny said. It wasn't so much of a question as a statement of fact. Larry couldn't disagree.

"Yeah, I guess so."

"Well listen, my pal from college is running for Governor. His name is Ed King. You heard of him?" Benny asked.

"Sure," Larry said. He had heard about this businessman who was raising lots of money in the Governor's race.

"We were on the football team together, Larry! He's in that team photo I gave you when you were a kid. He's number 34. Tough kid! He was a defensive end."

"No kidding?" Larry remembered the photo. He tried to

remember where he'd put it. Benny lowered his voice, something he only did when he was asking a favor.

"Would you be able to help him out up here in Methuen?" Benny asked.

"How can I help?"

"He's going to come up to the mall. You can walk him around and introduce him to people. Everyone knows you around here, right?"

Larry thought about it and decided, "Why not?"

He and Eileen spent the day with Ed King, introducing him to folks at the mall and seeing him shake hands and win votes. Ed King won the Democratic nomination that year and went on to become Governor. Larry and Eileen were invited to the Inauguration Ball. As they danced out onto the ballroom floor, they celebrated helping Benny out, and Governor King. Larry's eyes were opened to the challenges and promise surrounding campaigns and politics. Larry liked applying his competitive spirit to something new. He was always ready for a good fight.

The house on 60 Dean Street eventually emptied of everyone except for Helen. As the last of her foster children left, she found herself sitting alone on the porch with nobody to call home to dinner. There were no more skinned knees and bruises to clean up and bandage. There were no more grass-stained shirts to wash. An unexpected quiet descended upon her house. The green broom that had been the scourge of misbehaving children for decades rested against the inside of the closet, no longer needed.

Helen took in an apricot-colored poodle named Buffy. The excitable little dog would follow her everywhere, and the pair cut a fine figure walking the grounds around her house. Every Sunday, Helen left Buffy in the house and walked to church, waving occasionally to the neighbors who had also remained in their homes, and nodding politely to the new neighbors who had moved in. She came home from each service to find Buffy leaping for joy at the front window as she fumbled with her keys at the entryway.

This unexpectedly quiet life in the Swan Street Park neighborhood was interrupted frequently by visits from Helen's children and grandchildren. Once a week, Eileen and Larry would come and pick up Helen and Buffy for a daylong visit at their house in Methuen. Eileen would pour tea for mother and son as they sat and talked under the arbor leaves in the garden. When Larry had to go to work for the night shift, Helen would insist on helping Eileen with the cooking or the laundry, long after she had the capacity to keep working. Marie Jean always knew when her Nana had come up to the house for a visit during the school day, because she would find her socks neatly bundled together on her bed, though not a single bundle was a matching pair.

When the stairs on Dean Street finally got too steep, and the house on Dean Street was too far away for Rosemary or Larry to be close enough to help, Helen moved into Rosemary's house. She was there for three years as her grandkids kids grew up around her. Benny brought his family, and Larry and Eileen came to visit as often as they could. They enjoyed their time they had together as best they could as Helen's regular visits to the doctor became emergency trips to the hospital, and the care her family could provide in a home fell short of the care professionals could provide in a healthcare facility. The family made the somber and difficult decision to move Helen into a nursing home.

Larry took the day off work to pick up his mum from Rosemary's house. They drove together along the winding roads around Everett to the assisted living facility. Larry walked her inside and helped her check into the unit. They were introduced to the staff and passed the other residents. Larry and his mum sat together in the crisp cleanliness of her new living space. They spoke to each other the way they did when they were at Larry's home in Methuen, or Rosemary's yard in Melrose. When it was finally time for Larry to leave, he went to stand up. His mum lifted her hand uncertainly and said, "Wait."

"What is it, Mum?"

"Don't leave me here with the old people," she whispered.

Larry sat down and stayed a while longer, until the staff told him it was time to go. Then he walked himself along the leveled cement pathways to the parking lot, sat down in his car and cried. The thing he had worried about most was happening. She was being taken away from him.

In 1982 Larry received two important offers. First came a letter inviting him to coach the U.S. martial arts team in international competitions held in Taipei, China. The invitation came in recognition of his decades of experience studying and teaching karate.

And, in the process of securing his passport for travel, the State's newly renamed Department of Children and Families offered to help him contact his birth mother.

Larry went to China and coached the team. But he needed time to think about the second offer. He felt conflicted. He didn't want to confuse things or hurt the real parent who had sacrificed so much to care for him by going on a quest to find the birth parent who had abandoned him. He visited his mum in the nursing home, and they spoke about it. She saw the confusion in his eyes and nodded to him, rallying his confidence.

"Go ahead," she said. But she didn't want any details.

Larry was given the last known address for the woman on file as his real mother. It had come from handwritten correspondence with state agencies after she was deported. The letters had the name of that sweet-faced young woman who had left him in the hotel room in Springfield. His first letter reaching out to her went unanswered for months. He later learned that it had gone to another family member's address and had never reached his birth mother. Another letter was sent, and eventually it led to a phone call. Larry was fully prepared to hear the woman on the other end say she preferred not to talk to him. He knew it was possible that she might hang up on him. She didn't. Larry heard her voice on the other end of the line say "Hallo" in a Quebecois accent.

"Hello Marie Jean, my name is Larry Giordano, and I'm your son."

There was no shock in her voice, only the deep sadness of a life lived apart. She whispered the only thing she could think to say.

"I had to. I'm sorry. I hope she took good care of you ..."

She was talking to her son now, for the first time, after all these years ... hoping to be assured that another mother had done the work she couldn't. Visions of everything his mum had done for him flashed across Larry's mind. The first words that his biological mother had spoken to him made his foster mother's actions more tangible than ever.

"Yeah, she did take good care of me."

❖ ❖ ❖

Larry paid his mum a visit after work. This time she was at Wakefield Hospital. Larry navigated a maze of hallways and rode an elevator up three floors to her small room overlooking a strip of green space between rows of commuter brake lights snaking their way home after a long day of work. Larry sat beside his mum and held her hand, asking how she felt. She lied and said she was fine. He asked her what she needed. She told the truth and said nothing.

They talked about the kids, and how beautiful they were. Larry told her how his daughter, Marie Jean, ran like a gazelle and how his son, Lonnie, was so strong he could drag the barbecue across the deck outside. He showed her pictures of little Stephen. Helen smiled as the images of young Larry coursed through her waking memory: the little man off to play all day in the park; his long strides running through the door for dinner; his beaming smile after he dove into the lake during their summers in the New Hampshire cabin. She spoke about how beautiful her grandkids were and how proud of them she was, but what she meant was that those memories of their time together were precious, and how proud she was of him right now.

Helen lay quiet, looking comfortable and contented. Larry leaned forward, kissed her on the cheek and made his way back through the hallways, which at the moment felt as long and winding as their time together. Out of all the children Helen raised, her own and the ones she fostered, Larry was the last one to see her alive.

He received the call the next morning. He held the phone to his ear while the voice continued with, "I'm sorry" and "so difficult." The tears fell from his cheeks, partly out of sadness and partly from remembering what he had been able to tell his birth mother over the phone. He repeated it to himself now.

"Yeah, she did take good care of me."

Larry dancing with his mum, Helen Giordano, at his wedding

Benny Giordano giving a toast to Larry and Eileen at their wedding

Helen Giordano with Larry and Eileen's children, Lonnie and Stephen

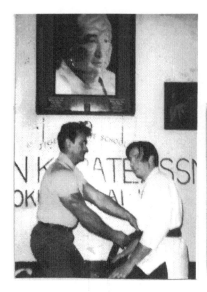

Larry during his black belt ceremony with Sensei Donald I. Buck (above left). training with Sensei Steve Senne (above right), and demonstrating tameshiwari brick breaking (below)

The Giordano family from left to right: Lonnie, Stephen, Marie
Jean, Eileen and Larry

The Giordano family from left to right: Stephen, Marie Jean,
Lonnie, Eileen and Larry

Epilogue

Larry and Eileen raised their family in Methuen, Massachusetts. The karate school grew to become a cornerstone business in the community, with Larry at the helm teaching generations of students. The child who had resisted any kind of discipline made teaching self-discipline his life's work. If his friends were surprised to see him become a firefighter in the Air Force, they were even more shocked to learn Larry became a longstanding member of the Methuen Police Force. The Swan Street Park Rat who had set traps for cops found himself in uniform and on patrol. Over the years, Larry was also elected to public office in several different capacities. The boy who grew up as a state ward became a successful state representative, advocating for Methuen in the Massachusetts State House.

Larry and Eileen carried that spirit of public service with them as they created a new nonprofit in the region—The Foster Kids of the Merrimack Valley—to support children facing challenges similar to those that Larry faced as a foster child. Larry didn't want to see another generation of foster kids carrying their belongings in garbage bags. He knew what it was like. But, he also knew unconditional love, and together, Larry and Eileen wanted the foster kids of the Merrimack Valley to know that, too.

Made in the USA
Middletown, DE
22 February 2019